BIGITY ANNE

HELEN F. DARINGER

ILLUSTRATED BY DON SIBLEY

HARCOURT, BRACE AND COMPANY, NEW YORK

CONTENTS

BIGITY ANNE

1

THE HOUSEKEEPER

While Mrs. Lloyd was not looking, Anne whittled one of the carrots she was scraping for the midday lunch to the sharp shape of Mrs. Lloyd's nose.

"If I knew where to find your brother David"—Mrs. Lloyd paused to count stitches in a doily she was crocheting—"I'd send him to the grocery store."

Anne said nothing. The housekeeper knew as well as she did that the boys went to play in the pasture every chance they had.

"What with four children in the house, anybody'd think it wouldn't be necessary for me to run errands," Mrs. Lloyd complained. "I s'pose I'll have to change out of my kitchen apron and go all the way down street myself for the onions."

Above the carrot nose Anne gouged out a hole to look like an eye. If she offered to go to the grocery store Mrs. Lloyd would find some excuse not to let her. Mrs. Lloyd enjoyed making trips to town.

"Alan and Jodie don't like onions," Anne couldn't help reminding her, although she knew it would do no good. "Alan won't touch the soup if there are onions in it."

Sometimes Mrs. Lloyd would do things for Alan she would not do for the others, but this was not one of the times. "Alan must learn to eat whatever's put upon his plate," she observed severely, "the same as I learned when I was Alan's size."

To imagine so big and bulky a woman reduced to the size of seven-year-old Alan required a little effort upon Anne's part, but the resultant dwarfed figure she beheld with her mind's eye was so wonderfully odd and funny she almost giggled out loud. For her imagination had suddenly reduced the housekeeper small as any circus midget, yet still complete with frizzly gray hair, frown-creased forehead, double chin, spotted blue apron and crochet hook.

"I must say I'm astonished at Rose Malet," the familiar complaint resumed at the other end of the kitchen table, "to realize how she pampered you children. You've got to learn the world's not made to your private order, no more than I hired myself out to cater to finicky whims and notions."

To keep herself from talking back, Anne concentrated upon a second eye for the carrot. All morning long she had been wishing that Mrs. Malet had not been obliged to go keep house for her sick daughter in Ohio. Anne even wished it were not vacation time, for if she were at school she would not be peeling potatoes and scraping carrots.

It was different with the boys. As soon as David had made his bed and helped Alan with his, the two were free to play provided they took five-year-old Jodie with them to keep her out from under Mrs. Lloyd's feet. But Anne was needed, Mrs. Lloyd declared; a girl who was in the eighth grade at school was plenty big enough to make herself useful at home.

It wasn't that Anne was unwilling to do her share. She used to enjoy assisting Mrs. Malet, but the new house-keeper never seemed to think you had things of your own to do. Nor did she ever say thank you when you had done what she said, or remark how nice the room looked now that you had straightened it up.

Mostly she just sat in the kitchen and crocheted, or leaned upon the fence to talk with the neighbors, or drew up a cushioned chair to a front window to watch who was passing by. She never baked cookies and she would not let Anne because she said it would make a mess in the kitchen. She never cooked anything that anybody liked, and even her mashed potatoes and gravy didn't taste good like Mrs. Malet's.

David, who was ten, had sent a letter to their father in Ecuador, asking him please to write back immediately to notify Mrs. Lloyd she was not to work for them any longer. David told him she would never let them have their own way about anything, and the only one she ever acted really nice to was Alan.

The only reason Mrs. Lloyd liked Alan, David went on to explain, was that she had not discovered what kind of boy Alan actually was. Because whenever she ordered Alan not to bring his jar of tadpoles into the house, or not to dig in the garden for worms, or not to play with Dinky Smith, Alan would put on such a dreamy, far-away expression she thought he was as innocent as he looked.

The funny thing was that she never noticed that right afterward Alan would take pains to do whatever she had told him not to. Sometimes it was even dangerous things he might not have thought of himself, like eating the dried-up bittersweet berries off the bouquet on the mantel. The berries must not be poison after all, though, because they had only given him a stomach-ache.

Reluctantly, and only because Anne could think up reasons faster than David could answer them, David had consented to add a postscript to his letter. If their father thought they ought to, he had promised in a sprawly, uphill sentence at the end, they would try to get along with the new housekeeper until Mrs. Malet returned.

In most arguments David was rather easily won over to Anne's side, but not this time. Not for a second did he believe it would make their father worry to know about Mrs. Lloyd. And why should anybody feel sorry for their father and try to keep him from worrying, just because the oil company had sent him so far away? David only wished he himself were one of the ten American engineers camping in a pathless forest where Indians still went about stark naked and hunted with poisoned arrows.

Nevertheless David had later unsealed the letter to add a second postscript of his own devising. He did not want his father to get the impression that he was not equal to coping with the new housekeeper when she acted cross. When you have a father who can make a road through an unbroken jungle and build bridges for rivers that come sliding down from the shining snow fields high on the Andes mountains, you must show what stuff you yourself are made of. Particularly if you are trying to persuade him to let you go with him to the jungle.

"P.S. No. 2," David scrawled in pencil on the back of the page. "Maybbe you better not let that same Inca Indain cary your letter down the mountains to the railroad stashun. He must lose them or something because we have not had one since before Christmas.

"Don't you worry about us, Dad. I and Anne are big enouff to look out for our own selves, and I already essplained how Alan does and if that cranky old Lilly Lloyd makes Jodie cry again I'll shure make her sorry."

Although Anne had warned David to remember how long it took a letter to reach their father—indeed, if the Indian runner was careless it might never reach the camp on the high plateau—she herself had begun within the week to inquire two or three times daily at the post office for mail. For almost a fortnight she hardly minded how much Mrs. Lloyd scorched the oatmeal and found fault with the children. Already, if Mrs. Lloyd but knew it, the days of her sway were numbered, her rule tottering.

But as April passed and then May, and still no reply had come from their father, Mrs. Lloyd had entrenched herself more and more solidly in command. For now Mrs. Malet's other daughter, the one who had twin babies and lived on a farm in Indiana, had fallen ill.

"On my way to the grocery store I may stop by to have

Fannie White show me that new crochet pattern she was telling about." The monotonous voice broke in on Anne's thoughts. Mrs. Lloyd heaved herself off the kitchen chair to untie her apron and run a hand over her frizzly hair to smooth it down. "Soon as you put the carrots into the soup kettle, Anne, I want you to clean off the kitchen table and set it ready for lunch.

"Nor don't let the soup stick and burn. Unless it's stirred, vegetable soup sticks awful easy." Mrs. Lloyd munched a few raisins to fortify herself for the journey down street. She was fond of raisins. "And I want you should rinse out the dishtowels I put to soak last night and hang 'em out to dry. I shan't be gone long, dependin' upon how complicated a stitch Lettie's new bedspread pattern is.

"And mind you now, you're not to begin to slacken up with your chores the minute you think my back is turned. Remember, Anne"—pointing a cautionary forefinger in Anne's direction for emphasis—"remember I don't hold with dawdling. You children must learn not to waste time. Are you paying attention to what I say, Anne?"

"Yes, Mrs. Lloyd, I heard you." Meekly respectful though the reply sounded, Anne's gray eyes under their dark lashes were sparkling like Alan's when he plotted

victory for some small private design of his own against the housekeeper's authority.

Anne did not dawdle. Quite the contrary. Before the housekeeper's voluminous blue-calico figure had proceeded a block down the street, Anne had dumped the cleaned carrots into the soup kettle, shoved the remainder back into the basket, cleared the kitchen table of vegetable peelings and the housekeeper's unwashed coffee-pot, and set out soup plates and spoons. Mrs. Lloyd did not believe in such extras as bread and butter plates and place mats; she believed the only time you needed such special fancy trimmings on the table was when there was company invited.

Scrupulous to neglect no detail of Mrs. Lloyd's parting instructions, Anne gave the kettle one brisk stir, flipping off the gas burner to make doubly certain the soup should not stick. Mrs. Lloyd would linger at least an hour at Mrs. White's, and probably longer—she always did. The carrots could cook with the onions after her return.

"How was I to know, Mrs. Lloyd?" With the ear of her mind, above the noise of the water with which she was splashing the soiled towels for a hasty rinsing, Anne could hear herself making reply to the housekeeper. She would speak in a voice so soft and innocent Mrs. Lloyd couldn't possibly accuse her of being impertinent.

"You didn't tell me to wash the towels. You only said *rinse*, Mrs. Lloyd, I remember distinctly. And you know you're trying to teach us to obey without asking any questions."

2

THE RESCUE

When Anne carried the dripping dishtowels outdoors she was surprised to see Jodie crouched beside the clothespole, her curly blond head half concealed below the housekeeper's flapping petticoats and long woolen underwear, hung out to sun before being packed away for the summer.

"I'm not Jodie, I'm a pwincess," the five-year-old announced. "A Inca pwincess wif heaps of tweasure we digged out of a secwet cave.

"The enemy's going to make a sacwifice of me and steal the gold," she continued happily. "But the Incas'll come and shoot 'em all dead wif poisoned awwows." She drew an imaginary bow to let fly an imaginary arrow.

"Den we'll wun quick to the jungle an' have a big jam-bowee, jus' like weal Indjuns."

"Aye, aye, your royal highness." Anne saluted the princess, at the same time extending the half empty box of raisins she had brought from the kitchen. "Your chief-tain sends this pemmican by secret messenger to stave off starvation until he can come to your rescue."

With quite unregal haste her royal highness plunged first one grimy little fist, then the other into the box to withdraw cram-full of sticky sweet fruit.

"Already your tribesmen are treading the war path," the messenger continued, dropping her voice to a sepul-chral whisper which made the princess shiver with ter-rified delight, it sounded so dreadfully dangerous. "Remember the password—*Revenge and rescue!*

"Don't wipe your hands on the front of your dress, Babe." For the moment Anne was merely big sister again. "Slilly Lloyd'll scold if you get your dress dirty." She shook a few more raisins into Jodie's cupped palms. "I'm going to the pasture to read."

Of all the books in the house, Anne liked *Little Women* best. Of course she would have preferred one she had not read so many times, but Mrs. Lloyd had taken away her library card. Mrs. Lloyd said reading was a waste of time.

Only since their mother's death three years ago had

the family lived in Springtown, with Mrs. Malet to run the house. Though Mrs. Malet occasionally got cross and peppery (all grown-ups do, Anne had observed), it never lasted longer than a few minutes. And she always made up for it afterward with a fresh batch of cookies or something extra special for dessert, caramel custard or floating island or whipped cream and jello.

When Father was about the age of David, Mrs. Malet used to be his grandmother's hired girl. She was not old enough then to be married, and everybody called her Rosie. When Father came to Springtown to visit his grandparents, Rosie would make all the things he specially liked—mashed potatoes and fried chicken and gravy, strawberry jam and applesauce and corn on the cob, and a whole big gallon freezer of homemade peach ice cream.

Father thought Springtown was a better place than the city to bring up a motherless family, and the children shared his opinion. For it was the kind of little town which is half country, with fields beginning right behind the houses and fruit trees growing in everybody's back yard.

There was even a creek meandering through the wide, wooded pasture which began where their yard left off, and an irregular hump of land which the boys called a hill, high enough to coast down in winter. Alan liked to stand on the hill to watch the trains go by. Whenever the boys played Indian, which was most of the time, it served as a look-out.

Anne was almost sorry she had outgrown the kind of game they were playing now, hiding behind bushes to dash out with whoops and yells, brandishing their home-made bows and arrows as they prepared for another fierce attack. Micky Moore used to praise Anne's aim as better than any fellow's in the whole gang, except of course his own. But Micky was fourteen now, and some of the others even older, and they could none of them afford any more than Anne to be seen playing such childish games.

Although Dinky Smith and both the Sage brothers were taller than David, he was captain of the eight or ten little boys who had inherited the pasture hunting-ground from their elders. He was a daring leader, expert in wilderness strategies, which no doubt was why his Inca tribesmen remained undisputed masters of the whole vast territory.

"Smear your arrows with poison, men," he directed as the army halted beside the creek.

For any notice they took of Anne, settling herself underneath a willow with her book, she might have been a thin green bush or a patch of shadow on the sunny grass.

"Rub the poison on good an' thick, men," David advised, plastering his own handful of alderbush arrows with black, oozy mud. "The enemy's drawn up in full force and this'll be the toughest battle yet.

"Sandy, you and Bim deploy 'round the enemy's rear so as we can attack on all sides at once. Butch, don't forget you're to rescue the princess and seize the gold." The youngest of the band, barely seven, Butch was more dependable as royal escort than as unerring marksman. "Remember, men, this is a surprise raid. Hold fire till I give the word."

Whether because of some vague premonition of hazards which the Incas could not foresee, or simply because she was in no mood to sit still and do nothing upon so bright and breezy a day, Anne slipped her book into a crotch of the willow and followed the warriors— at a discreet distance, certainly, not to attract attention— some yards behind Alan, who as usual was trailing far to the rear.

It was odd—she had noticed it more than once—but David always seemed to be in the midst of whatever excitement there might be, while Alan puttered along on the outskirts. It wasn't that Alan wasn't venturesome; he just seemed always to be thinking about something else. "Letting his wits go wool-gathering," Mrs. Malet called it, but she was sure he would outgrow it in good time.

There was a shrill shout of command from the chieftain, an answering chorus of war whoops from the Indians. Screaming and yelling, the band broke into a wild run which carried them safely beyond the last alder clump in the meadow.

Not until Anne saw them drop upon all fours to wriggle under the barbed-wire fence which kept the cows from getting into people's back yards, did she realize that David intended to lead the boys right up into the yard. . . . Boys were careless. It would never occur to David to warn them to keep clear of Mrs. Lloyd's clothesline.

Speedier than the gusty breeze which huffed and puffed at her back, Anne ran to intercept the children.

There was no telling what the housekeeper might do if they should happen to get mud on her clean clothes. She might even forbid David to play in the pasture again.

Had the shoulder of Anne's dress not caught upon the barbed wire as she crawled under, she might have caught up with the boys in time to cry caution.

Instead, pinned fast, she heard David's command to "Charge, fellows, charge!", heard the fierce howls and yelps of the embattled Indians, and just managing to raise her head a few inches, beheld them advancing upon the foe.

"Stop!" she shouted, and again as loudly as she was able, prone in the grass, "Stop it, boys!"

As well attempt with a spoken word to halt a swarm of mosquitoes. For the object of the Incas' desperate attack, as now she saw with helpless dismay, was none other than Mrs. Lloyd's clothesline of flannel petticoats and long-legged underwear, flapping and flopping in wild challenge to wind and warriors alike.

Within the instant a volley of poisoned shafts let fly at the insolent flannel foe, and then a second volley, at closer range, accompanied by such a fearsome din of hoots and screeches and shrill treble squeals as must have struck terror to the stoutest enemy.

"We've won, men, we've won!" cried the chieftain, loosing his last arrow at a quivering underwear leg. "Hurrah, hurrah!"

But from the ranks there arose no answering cheer. The victors had been stricken voiceless.

"What are you boys doing, I want to know?"

A thunderbolt falling into their midst would have taken them less by surprise, a fire-breathing dragon would have given them less occasion for alarm.

"Throwing mud on my clean clothes! So that's what you're up to, is it?" Mrs. Lloyd's broad face was red with anger, every ounce of her almost two hundred pounds vibrated with rage.

"Thought I wouldn't get back from the store in time to catch you at it! Surprised, ain't you?" When Mrs. Lloyd was exasperated she was prone to forget her grammar. "Caught you red-handed in the very act, didn't I?"

Helpless as a flock of small feathered birds hypnotized by the glittering eye of a jungle snake, the little boys stood paralyzed, unable either to move or speak. The very blades of grass trembled to hear the ominous thump-thump-THUD of the housekeeper's ponderous approaching feet.

"Just you wait, you wicked bad boys, just you wait! Your mothers'll hear about this! They'll spank you so hard you won't any of you be able to sit down for a week."

In vain Anne struggled to free herself. "Help me, Alan," she pleaded as he came lagging up, an arm's length away. "I'm caught."

Since he did not so much as glance in her direction, he may not have comprehended her plea. Or perhaps his mind was elsewhere as he flattened out to squirm under the fence.

"Let me loose, Alan, *please!*" she begged, again attempting to wriggle free. "Old Lloyd's so hopping mad I'm afraid she'll spank Jodie."

Still the boy gave no sign of hearing. Scrambling to his feet he paused for a moment to take account of the scene before him—the huddle of cowed, silent children and towering like fate above them, the imposing blue bulk of Mrs. Lilly Lloyd.

Almost inaudibly Alan began to intone to himself, "Mis' Slilly Lloyd, Mis' Slilly Lloyd, Mis' Slilly Slloyd." His bare feet under his muddy blue overalls began mechanically to chug-chug up and down, his sunburned arms alternately thrusting forward and pulling back, like well-oiled piston rods warming to their task.

"And if your mothers don't punish you boys as much as you deserve"—Mrs. Lloyd's voice was growing shriller and shriller—"I'll spank you myself! It's an outrage, that's what it is!

"You, David Todd, you march yourself straight into the kitchen and wait there till I come. I'll make a proper example of you, I will. This is the last time you'll be let run in the pasture, I tell you that right now.

"And look at you, Jodie! Dirt from head to foot! What did I tell you about keeping clean?"

"Alan, please, Alan!" cried Anne despairingly. "Don't go playing at engine now!"

But Alan was not playing at engine. For the moment he actually *was* an engine, iron-clad, vast and powerful.

"Mis' Slilly Lloyd, Slilly Lilly Lloyd, Slloyd-SLLOYD-SLLOYD!" With a horrid hooting sound from his whistle, he picked up steam and got under way. And the tracks upon which he had no choice but to run, led straight forward.

With a final frantic effort Anne wrenched the shoulder of her dress loose from the barbs, but only in time to see the blue-overalled figure of her little brother drive headlong on, past the sagging clothespole and the sobbing Jodie, past the forlorn squad of Indians and the mud-spattered underwear legs dangling from the line. Betwixt him and the grim-faced housekeeper there remained no more than a brief margin of grassy lawn.

"Alan!" Anne shouted at the top of her voice as she raced after him. "Alan Todd, be careful!"

"SLILLY LLOYD, SLILLY LILLY, SILLY LILLY, SLLOYD SLLOYD!" With a prolonged series of fearsome hoots to clear the tracks, the locomotive swept unswerving on.

At first startled, then alarmed, at the sight of the small fair-haired figure driving straight at her, Mrs. Lloyd half lifted a hand to stop him, realized it was too late, and ignominiously gave ground.

The unseemly haste of her sideward hop made the little boys grin and titter, and the sound of their own giggles restored them to themselves.

"Tell my mother for all I care," Dinky Smith shrilled at the housekeeper as he took to his heels. "My mother never spanks me no matter what I do."

Emboldened, reckless, the others laughed out loud to

see Mrs. Lloyd shake her fist at Dinky's retreating rear, and some even went so far as to stick out their tongues and make faces at her before they withdrew to safer ground.

"You'll pay dear for this, young lady," the housekeeper threatened Anne. "It's all your fault and David's. I'll punish you proper, both of you, that I will! and Jodie too, muddying herself up when I told her not to." But for some reason the loud voice was less fearsome than it might have been. The threat sounded like bluster.

"You're not permitted to lay hands on us," Anne boldly reminded her. "Mrs. Malet said you weren't."

"No back talk from you, young lady Todd, I won't put up with it!" the housekeeper shouted, regardless of dignity.

"Young man, trot yourself right back this instant into the house till I can tend to you!" For David, heartened by echoes of Indian catcalls from the far side of the fence, had plucked up courage to creep forth from his place of banishment.

"As for you, Jodie Todd—"

"You're discharged, Mrs. Lloyd." Though it was Anne who spoke, she was almost as startled as Mrs. Lloyd herself to hear the pronouncement. It was as if, suddenly and quite unexpectedly, the words had uttered themselves.

"I discharge you right now, for keeps." This time Anne knew exactly what she was saying. And something in the steadiness of her gray-eyed gaze, in the stubborn quiet of her voice, must have convinced the housekeeper that the dismissal was final.

"Well, I never! No, I never did. Such ungrateful children I never did see—no, never," she declared, uncertain whether she ought to feel sorry for herself or outraged. "After all these weeks I've slaved to make you comfortable, this is my reward."

"Good-bye, Mis' Lloyd." It was Alan, looking up at her with such an appealing air of innocence, his eyes so blue, his tousled head so golden in the sun, she thought for a moment of taking him away with her, out from under the evil influence of his elder brother and sister. Poor harmless little fellow, she was sure he was not to blame for what had happened.

"I wouldn't stay another day in this house," Mrs. Lloyd proclaimed for all the world to hear, "no, not for a million dollars."

"Don't think you've heard the last of this, Anne Todd," she turned again to threaten in a loud voice from the kitchen door. "Before the week is out, you'll have cause to rue this day." The screen door slammed behind her.

"Old Lloyd can't scare us," asserted David, trying to

look brave. "She can't do anything to us, can she, Anne?"

And because Anne heard the quaver in David's voice and saw the tears still wet on Jodie's dirt-streaked cheeks, she made her reply sound far more bold and cheerful than she felt. "Of course she can't scare us! We won't let her. Besides, she's already discharged and packing up her belongings to go.

"Alan"—beckoning him close to whisper in his ear, but careful that the other two could overhear—"do you s'pose you could sneak in by the front door and get the money we were saving for the circus out of my bottom drawer? We'll all go down to the drugstore and have an ice-cream soda until Slilly Lloyd's gone."

"I'm going to have a banana split," David declared, puffing out his chest, "with two scoops of ice cream and a cherry on top of the whipped cream. Oh, boy!"

"Me too, me too," echoed Jodie with a squeal of pleasure. "Chocklit wif a chewwy on top!"

3

CONSEQUENCES

"Careful, David," cautioned Anne. "It's heavy. Don't drop it."

Mounted upon a chair David reached on a pantry shelf for the yellow-painted cookie-jar in which Mrs. Lloyd had kept the money for the household expenses.

When the top was lifted off, however, with Alan and Jodie crowding close for coins to fetch a loaf of bread and a can each of pineapple and baked beans from the grocery store for supper, the jar proved to be empty. Empty, that is, except for a scrap of paper torn from the top of a paper bag.

"I am entitled to a month's pay in advance because you did not give notice." The handwriting was Mrs.

Lloyd's, almost as uneven and uphill as David's own. "It's mine by rights, so I am taking it." Although the message was unsigned, there was no need for signature.

"She's no right to the money," David declared indignantly. "It belonged to us and she had no right to take it."

Alan stood upon the rung of a chair to see for himself the emptiness within the yellow crockery jar. "Will they make us go to live in the poorhouse?" he questioned uneasily, sensing the dismay and uncertainty which darkened Anne's gray eyes and wrinkled her brow. "Will we starve, Sister, 'cause there's no money left to buy with?"

It was almost the same question Anne was asking herself, for the moment completely at a loss for an answer. They must not go into debt—that was one of the things she and Mrs. Malet had promised Father—nor could they draw money from the bank because that must be saved for illnesses and emergencies. Yet it would be at least a week before the July check came from the oil company.

"Don't worry, we'll get along somehow, all of us together," Anne promised, trying to sound as soothing and comfortable as Mrs. Malet when one of the children fell ill. "Just think how lucky we are to be rid of Mrs. Lloyd!"

Whether it was the reassuring sound of her own voice which restored Anne's confidence, or that she knew the children depended upon her because she was the oldest, she was already beginning to think how to manage. When you have two younger brothers and a little sister to be responsible for, you must learn to make the best of whatever happens.

"There are some canned things in the pantry and there's still a dollar left of my circus money. When that's spent we'll use what's in the three piggy-banks."

David's face clouded. For weeks he had been denying himself candy and ice-cream cones, hoarding every penny of his ten-cent allowance as well as what Mrs. Scott next door paid him to rake her lawn and run errands, in order to buy himself a nail-studded holster like the one Dinky Smith's aunt had sent Dinky for his birthday.

"You can have all what's saved in my pig, Anne," Alan made offer, plainly aware of the good example he was setting the other two children.

"Only I don't b'lieve my pig's got as much in it as Dave's," he admitted sweetly, with a sidelong glance at his elder brother, whose deepening gloom filmed his brown eyes with mist and beclouded even the drift of freckles on his snub nose. "Is Dave going to let you take his money, Anne?"

"Mine too." Whatever Alan did, Jodie always wished to do too. "My piggy too, ev'wy penny what's in it."

"I'll bet there's not more than two cents in Al's bank,"

David muttered with a scowl, "an' maybe not even two, because he always spends it as soon as he gets it. It's not fair." His voice was choky. "If I had my way Old Lilly Lloyd'd be locked up tight in jail where she couldn't ever get out. She's a regular old burglar, she is, and I'll tell her so to her face if ever I see her again, old cheater silly Lilly."

"Sh—sh, you mustn't call her names, Davie, it's not nice," Anne chided him, although privately she thought Mrs. Lloyd deserved it. "Think what fun it's going to be now that she's gone."

Then, as David still refused to smile, Anne remembered about Dinky's nail-studded leather holster. "Of course we'll repay the pigs the minute the oil check arrives," she assured him, and felt more cheerful herself to see his face brighten a little.

"Alan, you and Jodie take the onions Mrs. Lloyd bought back to the store and ask Mr. Snow please to give you a loaf of bread in exchange. We'll heat up the soup again and make believe we're Incas holding a pow-wow how to replenish our supplies.

"How's the hunting, Chief?" The query was directed at David, to take his mind off his grievances against the departed housekeeper. "What about shooting us a buffalo?"

"Not buffalo, that's not what Incas hunt." Although

David's accents were still somewhat froggy he was sufficiently himself again to have a woodsman's regard for accuracy. "It's wildcats and panthers. There's not any buffaloes in jungles."

Anne lighted the gas under the soup. "It'd be a tight squeeze for a panther in our kettle," she noted. "Would you just as lief make it a rabbit, Chief?"

He pretended to take the suggestion seriously. "I'll have to put it up to the tribe to see what they want." But as his eyes met hers he grinned. Unless David was upset about something, you could count upon him to meet you half way.

It was not until Anne was washing dishes, with Jodie and David drying them and Alan setting them away upon the shelves, that anyone remembered that tomorrow was circus day. Alan announced that he would have to go extra early to get a seat where he could watch exactly how they did the tight-wire bicycle act in the picture on the billboard—Dare-Devil Tony and two other men in purple tights.

Alan intended to stretch a clothesline across the back yard, from fence post to post, to practice on. Of course at first he would not string the rope very high, he explained, because if his bicycle happened to fall it might get scratched. He meant to take good care of his bicycle, not let it get all banged up like Dinky Smith's.

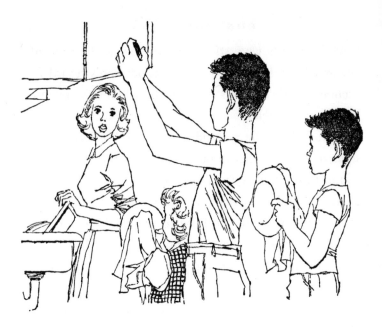

"Your bicycle, did you say? You're going to keep the 'namel shiny new?" David repeated after him in a superior, grown-up tone. "Don't talk through your hat, Al. Since when have you got a bicycle, I'd like to know?"

"I've almost got one," retorted Alan, flopping the wet end of his dishtowel as though by accident against his brother's chin. " 'Cause soon as Father comes home I mean to ask him to buy me one. I bet you a million dollars—"

"You don't have a million. You don't have even one dollar."

"Don't argue, boys." Anne emptied the dishwater

into the sink with such a sudden loud splash the two were startled into silence. "Have you forgotten there's no money for circus tickets?"

Unwilling to credit their own ears, the boys stared first at her, then at each other, their faces uncommonly solemn.

"But I have to go to the circus," protested David. "I already told the other fellows I am. Everybody's going, even Butch and Sandy, aren't they, Al?"

"A parade is practically the same as a circus, and it's free," Anne pointed out, determined for the children's sake to make the best of things, however disappointed she herself might be. "We can see the circus next summer when Father's here."

It was not every year that a circus came to town. Nor was tomorrow's exhibition to be one of those shabby, second-rate affairs with scarcely any clowns and only one ring, which are commonly the portion of little country places like Springtown. But even if it were to have been a mere third-rate performance, one to which their more experienced friends might have referred with scorn as "one-horse" and "half-pint," they still would not have been willing to miss it.

"I don't want to see it next summer, I want to see it now," David growled, slapping down his dishtowel.

"Maybe I'll use the money I saved and go. I can too, if I want to. It's my money."

He was not really defying her, Anne knew, it was only that he felt so stricken he had to talk big and unmanageable in order to keep his self-respect. She could sympathize with him. She too felt cheated and gloomy, except that, being the oldest, she couldn't give way to her disappointment.

Tomorrow the "Greatest Show on Earth" would pitch its tents in Springtown. Tomorrow all who had cash to purchase tickets would see revealed the wonders which billboards and bright-hued posters had for weeks been blazoning forth. There would be a galaxy of marvels—lordly wild beasts and lion tamers who thought nothing of sticking their heads down a lion's throat; a man with hair long as a woman's who could swallow a whole sword except the handle; midgets no bigger than Hop o' My Thumb. There was a lady with yellow curls who twice a day was shot out of the mouth of a cannon, just like a cannon ball. There were artists of the trapeze and aerial riders on tight-wires, and there were horses that danced and seals which beat the drum and played horns in a brass band. But perhaps most enthralling of all would be the platoon of clowns with baggy trousers and red-and-white-painted faces, so comical you had to laugh every time you saw their pictures on the poster in Mr. Snow's grocery store window.

"I wants to see the efalunts," whimpered Jodie, her face screwing up to cry. "You said you'd take me, Anne, an' now you won't."

"Don't fret yourself, Babe, you'll see elephants, lots of them, marching two by two along Main Street and right around the Square. And a calliope too"—Anne put as much enthusiasm as she could into the description— "a calliope 'most as big as this kitchen, playing tunes like a pipe-organ, only lots louder and livelier." Had it not been for the contrary example set by the two boys, it would have been easy to cajole Jodie into being satisfied with the parade.

"What does *rue-the-day* mean?" Alan inquired a little later, pronouncing it as though it were all one word. He seemed to be following some train of thought of his own. "Do you know what I think? *Can't-go-to-the-circus* is what I think.

"'Cause why?" With a knowing wag of the head he supplied the answer to his own question. "'Cause that's 'zackly what ole Mis' Lloyd said—*rue-the-day!*"

Anne had supposed that she alone remembered the housekeeper's warning, to be troubled by it. Generally Mrs. Lloyd's threats had been only ordinary, nothing to worry yourself about, no matter how rebellious her

bossy way of speaking to you might make you feel. Sometimes she had threatened to hold back their allowances
until they did as they were told, or she refused to let
them play with other children and wouldn't let them
have any jam for their bread because she said they didn't
deserve it.

The warning she had issued today, however, had been
of a different variety. Indeed had she been the wife of
an ogre in a fairy-story she could scarcely have acted
more spiteful. . . . But if Alan's interpretation was cor-
rect, why, then, Anne told herself, there was nothing to
be uneasy about. And how else could the housekeeper
get even with them, except by taking their money so they
could not attend the circus? It was just what you might
have expected from a person like Mrs. Lloyd.

"I'll show old Lloyd she can't interfere with me,"
David asserted, squaring his shoulders and lifting his
chin. "I'll carry water for the animals. That's how Micky
Moore's going to pay his way into the big tent, he told
me so himself. It'll take more than one boy to water all
the horses in a great big circus like that. I'll bet anything
Micky'll be glad to let me help him."

Anne might have reminded David that Micky was
four years older than he, and head and shoulders taller,
but she didn't. Nor did she tell him that there would be
others besides him and Micky seeking to earn admission,

and that the younger you are the less your chance of being selected. When your brother stiffens his knees and throws back his cropped brown head like a pony pulling himself together to make his way past some obstacle looming in the road, you only wish you could make it easier for him.

It was David himself, however, who felt it necessary to discourage Alan. "You're not old enough, Al," he told him, not unkindly. "A water bucket would be too heavy for you to lift unless it was only half filled. Maybe they'll pay me two tickets, and if they do, you can have the other one."

Anne swept the kitchen so she wouldn't have it to do in the morning. She wished she were a boy, able to earn a ticket for herself and Jodie. Jodie and Alan were too young to realize what marvelous things they would be missing—three different rings with three different performances all going on at once, and in the middle a big stage with acrobats and jugglers. All the while there would be clowns wandering in and out, pretending they didn't know it was a circus and tripping over their own feet when they tried to get out of people's way. Sometimes they would run to catch a ride in a funny old red automobile which the minute they climbed into it would roll over and spill them out into the sawdust. Sometimes one of the clowns might stop stock-still in front of your tier of seats to look up at you and wave, and you would wave back and everybody supposed of course he must be acquainted with you.

And always just before the end there came the most exciting thing of all—the horses with the bareback riders. If Anne could have her choice of what she would like to be, and if she hadn't David and Alan and Jodie to be responsible for, she would be a bareback rider. It was one of her favorite things to imagine before she went to sleep at night.

Sometimes she saw herself poised like a ballet dancer upon a fleet Arabian stallion, sometimes she imagined herself curtseying with effortless grace from the back of a swift-pacing palomino, to the applause and cheers of a thousand spectators. . . . Thinking about tomorrow, she had to sweep with all her might to keep from feeling sorry for herself. It made her heart thump just to imagine the circus horses, so proud and strong and beautiful.

David carried the alarm clock upstairs with him. "It's underneath my pillow so as not to wake Al," he explained when Anne stuck her head in at the door somewhat later to make sure the boys were not getting into bed partly dressed. "Al doesn't have to get up early like me, because the parade doesn't start until ten o'clock."

"I do too have to get up early," Alan mumbled from the other bed, his nose buried against the pillow. "I have to be up as early as Dave."

Anne did not contradict him. She thought he must be almost asleep.

4

MR. STOCKY

David must not have waited for the alarm to sound the next morning. The first thing Anne heard was the squeaky sound the stairs made as he went tiptoeing down in the dark before dawn. By the time she had put on some clothes to follow him he was standing at the kitchen door with his cap on.

He had no time for breakfast, he insisted, and he was not hungry. "Drink the milk while I cook you an egg and make some toast," she told him firmly. "It won't take a minute. Micky Moore won't even be awake yet, pitch dark as it is."

Before he left the house she stuffed two peanut-butter sandwiches into his pockets. "One's for Micky," she said.

"By the middle of the morning you'll be hollow as drums, working so hard."

Anne and Jodie would have gone downtown at nine o'clock, in case the parade should begin ahead of time, except that they could not find Alan. After breakfast he had taken David's lasso outdoors to practice, but when Anne went to the porch to summon him to wash his hands and change into a clean shirt he had disappeared.

He wasn't next door at Mrs. Scott's nor at any other neighbor's house, nor even at Dinky Smith's where Anne sent Jodie to inquire for him. Nor could Anne locate him in the pasture, though she went as far as the alder clump, looking and calling his name. She was loath to go without him, but perhaps he would remember about the parade in time to see at least part of it. Most likely he was scooping out a pond for minnows or digging a hole for a rabbit or chipmunk to use for a house. Though it would be nobody's fault but his own if he remembered too late, she would have searched until she found him except that it would not be fair to make Jodie miss the procession on his account.

The whole of Springtown had turned out to see the parade, and families had driven in from the country and neighboring towns as well. Anne had to take Jodie's hand to keep from losing her in the crowd on Main Street, especially as they approached the Square. It was like a Fourth of July Sunday-school picnic for excitement, with colored balloons flying on long strings and the sunshine so bright and everybody glad.

There was an agreeable smell of hamburgers frying in a canvas booth on the corner, of oranges and lemons being squeezed, of country dust and of brick pavements heating in the sun. Peddlers hawked cowboy hats and red-white-and-blue whirligigs that buzzed in the breeze. Boys wormed their way through the crowds to dash out into the middle of the street to observe whether the procession was yet in sight. When they said it wasn't, the grown people all began to talk to each other again about how much the gardens needed rain and the high prices the merchants charged and wasn't it a good thing it wasn't going to rain today because the children would have been so disappointed!

Jennie Allen had saved a place for Anne in front of Mr. Allen's real estate office. If there had been time Anne would have told her about the spiteful way Mrs. Lloyd had chosen to get even because they would not let her keep house for them any longer. Jennie Allen would certainly have sympathized, as she didn't like Mrs. Lloyd a bit better than Anne did. There was no time for talk, however. Hardly had Anne maneuvered Jodie into position between her and Jennie when there was a shout of

"It's coming!" and a gang of boys came galumphing down the street, noisy as school let out.

Unmistakable and clear, and growing louder every minute, the sound of music broke upon the air, bugles and trumpets, the clash of cymbals and *ratatatat, rubadubdub* of marching drums. Anne drew a deep breath and let the sounds sink into her, patterned like skyrockets and Roman candles, dazzling the darkness of her inner mind. Oh, to be a trumpeter blowing a bright brass horn, or play the stops of a piccolo to summon tunes like fountains of quicksilver! She had not heard a brass band for so long she had all but forgotten the splendor of the music.

Now a caravan began to roll past, red vans and white, with carved and gilded paneling, painted with life-sized pictures of the wild animals caged within, lions and tigers and spotted leopards, polar bears on blocks of ice and laughing hyenas with slinking tails, more different kinds of animals than in a zoo. Now there was a blue van with the sides let down so everybody could have a look at the hairy orangutan pressing his leathery face against the iron bars.

"BIGGEST in CAPTIVITY," the sign read. If only Alan were there to see the orang too! More than anything else in the world Alan liked live animals, even when they were only worms and caterpillars.

"Efalunts," squealed Jodie, "efalunts wif twunks!" And again, hopping up and down on one foot, "A efalunt wif a chair on his back!"

"That's a palanquin, Babe." Anne remembered the picture in the geography book although she was not quite sure how to pronounce the word. "That's the way kings and rich people ride in India."

But Jodie was not listening. "Look, Anne, look! A baby efalunt! He's got a chair on his back too," she noted with satisfaction, "and the man's only little too, like the efalunt."

"He's a boy," said Jennie Allen, "a boy not much bigger than you, Jodie. Most likely it's the snake charmer's little boy from India, his skin's so dark."

"Alan!" Jodie gave a shrill yelp. "Here I is, Alan, here I is!" If Anne had not been quick to jerk her back upon the sidewalk the child would have dodged out into the street, into the path of the ponderous, swaying elephants. "Let go of me, Anne. I wants to go wif Alan."

"Do you want an elephant to step on you?" Anne gave her a little shake to bring her to her senses. "Stand still and stop pulling, else I'll have to take you home."

Jodie strained to jerk loose from Anne's protective grip. "Alan!" she yelled, her childish treble breaking into a wail of disappointment as the pygmy elephant drew de-

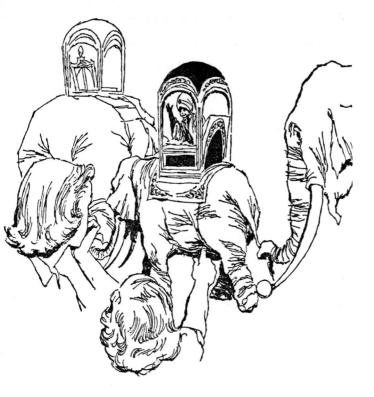

liberately past them, swinging his long trunk from side to side. "Look, Anne, look!"

Anne looked. To her amazement she saw that the snake charmer's little boy had turned to wave at them. At first her eye took in no more than the bespangled velvet palanquin in which he sat enthroned, the gold and scarlet of his embroidered coat. Then her eyes met his, startlingly blue in the dark bronze of his face, under the twisted folds of his turban.

She gasped. It couldn't be, it couldn't possibly be—but she was practically sure it was!

"Alan," she called, joining her voice in duet with Jodie. "Alan Todd!"

There was no reply. Pygmy elephant and palanquin and bronze-skinned, turbaned boy had rounded the corner, out of sight.

It was difficult to convince Jennie Allen, but once convinced, she was far more positive than Anne that the elephant boy could indeed have been no other than Anne's little brother. "They'll kidnap him," she prophesied darkly. Nor would she be budged from her opinion by Anne's protest that circuses don't steal children.

"Of course they won't call it that." Jennie gave her stubby brown braids an ominous shake. "They know good and well that kidnapping is against the law. But that's what it'll amount to, whatever they call it.

"They'll offer to let him ride the elephants as much as he wants and have a monkey for a pet and things like that, so they can say he went of his own free will. I shouldn't be s'prised if he even learned to be a lion tamer."

It was a possibility too dire to be brushed aside. In spite of trying not to, Anne found herself thinking of one reason after another to believe that Jennie might be better informed about such things than she herself was.

It would be easy to entice Alan. He was too young to have good judgment, especially if the animal trainer promised him a live pet. And he wouldn't realize until it was too late that they might not be willing to let him go home again.

"Come, Jodie." Anne seized her by the hand. "We must hurry as fast as we can to the circus grounds to get there before the parade. Alan's got to come right home with us."

Jennie was eager to accompany them, but first she must get permission from her father in the real estate office.

"I can't wait. It's too important," Anne told her, already beginning to elbow her way through the crowd. "Maybe you can catch up with us. Hold tight to my skirts, Jodie, not to lose yourself."

Under any circumstances it would have been a long walk from the Square to the field on the other side of town where the circus was set up. But this morning, with so many people on the sidewalks getting into the way and Jodie falling behind so often and having to be waited for, it seemed miles and miles. Anne's legs began to feel the way they did in a bad dream when she tried to run and couldn't lift her feet.

Even after she and Jodie reached the circus grounds they had to keep walking and walking. The parade had arrived ahead of them. Some on one side of the field, some on the other, vans were already being covered with canvas in readiness for the trip to the next town. Anne inquired of a man who was lacing a tarpaulin where the elephants were kept.

"You'll have to ask someone who tends the critters, Sister," he advised. "I'm only a roustabout. I wouldn't know."

Hot and dusty, Anne and Jodie plodded on across the field. Anne felt sorry for Jodie, her face looked so red, her forehead and short upper lip beaded with little drops of perspiration, and she was trying so valiantly not to drag behind. But until Alan had been found they could neither of them afford to take a minute's rest, no matter how out of breath and weary they were.

Had it not been that her mind was heavy, Anne would have enjoyed herself. It would have been fun to watch the circus hands drive iron stakes to set up the tents and then heave at the ropes like sailors in a motion picture. She could have stood for hours beside the lifted canvas of the horse tent, watching the attendants brush the glossy manes and tails and rub down the slender ankles in pails of clean soapy water.

And the cook tent was wide open too, for anyone to see inside. Rows of hungry men perched on high stools at long tables, spreading the piled pancakes on their plates with yellow butter and dousing them with brown syrup until the strings of sizzling little sausages at the side, and even the fried eggs, floated upon a pond of shallow sweetness. It must be a late breakfast some of the workers were having, Anne thought.

There was to be baked ham for lunch, she noticed. Dozens of hams were turning with a delectable flavorous odor on long spits at electric grills at the far end of the tent, and helpers were peeling potatoes and topping carrots and cutting onions and mixing what must be spice-cakes, or maybe puddings, in white bowls almost big enough to take a bath in.

"I'm hungwy, I wants sumfin to eat." Jodie eyed the mounds of pancakes and lifted her small round nose to sniff the blended fragrance of hot stew and ham and sausage.

"Be a good girl, Jodie, and wait till we get home." If Anne had had a nickel she'd have bought the child a bun. "It won't be long now. We'll soon find Alan."

None of the two or three men to whom Anne put her query could inform her where the elephants were, and one a little farther on, an ill-natured fellow with an ugly red scar across his face, told her not to try to bum her way in, buy a ticket like other people. The affront made her cheeks burn deeper red than his scar, but she bit her lip and held her tongue and kept her chin in the air and pretended she had not even heard how insulting he was.

It was some minutes before she inquired of anyone else. The men were so busy maybe she ought not bother them.

"Are you two children lost?" a stout man wanted to know, mopping his forehead with the back of his hand. He seemed to be a kind of foreman.

"Oh, no, sir, but my little brother is. I'm almost sure he's in with the elephants." Anne spoke very fast not to use up any more of the man's time than was necessary. "He's got blond hair and he's only seven years old."

The foreman seemed not to consider the situation unusual. "Never was a circus yet that a few children didn't get separated from their families. That's right, Sissie"— making pretense to nip Jodie's nose between thumb and forefinger—"hold on tight to big sister here and mind what she tells you.

"Hi, Peters," he shouted to a round-shouldered man who was swinging a water-can to and fro to settle the dust, "take these two kids over to Stocky in the animal tent. They think their little brother's got lost there.

"If you don't find him, Sister, just let me know." And before Anne could say "Thank you" he had turned to give orders to a crew of roustabouts.

It was no distance at all to the animal tent. Although

it was dim inside after the glare of the sun, with two or three rows of cages with animals blocking the view, Anne spied the elephants almost immediately. "I'm much obliged to you, Mr. Peters," she thanked him politely. "Don't let me keep you any longer from your work."

Mr. Peters, however, was in no haste to return to his sprinkling can, though she would have been more than a little relieved to have him depart. For suddenly, now that they were approaching closer and closer to the elephants —the huge grayish leathery bodies with legs thick as posts, the long, flexible trunks leisurely reaching out to gather up the freshly piled hay into neat little bundles to feed themselves—suddenly Anne realized she must have been mistaken. It couldn't have been Alan in the parade, not possibly.

If only she had used her head and reasoned, instead of getting excited! Right this minute Alan was prob-ably milling around on the Square with Dinky Smith, with his face not washed and still wearing yesterday's shirt. Provided, that is, that he wasn't still grubbing in the meadow. Whatever would Mr. Peters think of her, putting him and the foreman to so much trouble, and all for nothing?

"Hi there, Stocky, you busy?" Mr. Peters hailed a stooping figure which, unfolding gradually like a jack-knife, raised a grizzled head to greet them. "Here's a couple of kids lookin' to locate their brother that's went and losted hisself. The boss said fetch 'em to you.

"This here's Stocky, like I said," Mr. Peters introduced him to Anne. "Kingpin of the greatest show on earth, he is," he boasted, proud to claim acquaintance with so important a personage. "What Stocky don't know about handlin' wild beasts ain't worth knowin', eh, Stocky, ain't that so?

"Tell him your story, little girl, how come you think your brother was headin' for the ellyfunts when he disappeared."

Anne's throat was dry, her face hot with embarrassment to think how foolish she had been. Worse than foolish, it had been downright wrong of her to suspect a person like Mr. Stocky of being a kidnapper. Just to look at him you could see how nice he was, the quiet way he motioned Jodie not to be afraid to come up close to the elephants, he wouldn't let them hurt her. How could you ever explain to him? And what would he think?

"Did you see me, Anne, did you and Jodie see me in the parade?" A head poked out from behind an adjacent wooden cage, the head of a small boy with rumpled straw-colored hair and a face as brown as a coffee-bean.

"Why didn't you get here quicker, Anne, to see me 'fore I took off my circus suit?" He stepped out into the open to hitch his overalls higher and button up his shirt.

"Did you see me wave at you?" Alan almost never got excited the way Anne and David did, but he was beside himself with excitement now, puffing and swaggering like a bantam cock.

"I rode all by myself on top of an elephant, didn't I, Stocky? Nor the man that walked on the ground didn't have to use his stick once, 'cause I knew how to ride so well. Nabob's a fine elephant, isn't he, Stocky? And I'm a fine rider, amn't I, Stocky?"

Like an India-rubber ball jerked by a string Jodie bounced toward him. "I saw you, Alan!" she panted admiringly. "I saw you widin' on a efalunt. I wants to wide too, my own self." Forgetting in the eagerness of her desire to be timid with strangers, "Please, Mr. Efalunt Man," she appealed to Stocky, "I wants to wide too."

"Sh, Jodie, you mustn't bother Mr. Stocky." Anne was embarrassed. "He's busy."

"Bless my socks, so little Goldilocks has got her heart set on bein' an animal trainer just like her brother!" Stocky assumed such a comical expression Anne had to laugh.

"It beats the Dutch, it sure does. Must be there's circus blood in the family, is the only way I can figure it out. Your pappy doesn't chance to be a lion tamer, I suppose?" He winked at Anne so she would know he was only joking. And still wearing that droll, astonished ex pression that a child as young as Jodie should wish to mount an elephant, he whisked her off her feet to deposit her, giggling with half-scared delight, upon the broad back of the pygmy Nabob.

Anne longed to sit beside Jodie, if only for one minute, so she could tell Jennie Allen and the other girls she had. It would be even more wonderful than to ride a mettlesome palomino. An elephant, a real, live elephant from India! But she couldn't ask Mr. Stocky to let her, and she was so much bigger than the other two children that of course he would never think to offer.

"It'll take soap to get that stuff off," Stocky advised as he saw her attempt to rub some of the brown off Alan's face with a handkerchief. "Plenty of soap and warm water. It's the stuff young ladies paint their arms and legs and faces with to look like seashore beauties.

"Just a minute, young man." He laid a hand upon Alan's shoulder as the children turned to depart. "Aren't you forgetting something?"

Now that he was reminded, Alan remembered upon what important business he had set off alone for the circus grounds soon after breakfast. "The ticket. You said maybe you'd pay me a ticket." With all that had happened during the past three or four hours, the circus performance in the big tent had almost slipped his mind.

Anne took advantage of the delay to tuck Alan's shirt in at the rear where it was hanging out.

"Some such bargain as that I believe we struck," Stocky agreed. He took a pad of yellow paper and a pencil from his hip pocket. "The greatest show on earth holds to its bargains, come rain or shine. Now let me see what it tots up to."

He cogitated, chewing the end of his pencil. "Shining my shoes, that's worth something. Fetching me a plug of tobacco from the commissary, that's worth something. And substituting at the last minute for a dwarf who didn't know any better than to gorge himself on sausages and pancakes till his poor stomach couldn't abide the prospect of jogglin' up and down in a swaying palanquin— Well, that's worth a little something too.

"The way I figure it, young man"—Stocky scratched his grizzled head and made some scrawly pencil marks upon the yellow pad—"it adds up to one whole pass and a half.

"Take this piece of paper to the fellow at the wicket, and see you don't lose it on the way. It's a voucher, good for three half-passes to the afternoon performance in the big tent. One for you, one for Goldilocks, and one for your big sister."

The lump of disappointment which clogged Anne's throat was so hard and rough it made her eyes smart.

. . . A half-price ticket! She'd have to stay at home by herself. Jodie and Alan could go to the circus but she was over age. But she must thank Mr. Stocky anyhow; she mustn't hurt his feelings.

It must have been that Stocky had power to read the thoughts in people's minds, or at least Anne had reason to believe so. For as she was trying to clear her throat to say good-bye, he explained something she had not understood.

"Passes aren't like tickets, dependin' upon your age. They go more by how big you are," he remarked casually. "Ain't that so, Peters?"

Mr. Peters allowed that it certainly was so.

"Oh, thank you, Mr. Stocky!" The knot in Anne's throat having quite melted away, her words came out clear and glad. "We're all of us ever so much obliged to you, heaps and heaps!"

"No thanks to me, Sister. It's Al here. He earned the passes. Come around again next year, Al, when the big show puts in. Likely there'll be a job waitin' for you."

5

THE POLICEMAN

The morning after the circus, when Anne said it had been such a long time since Mrs. Lloyd had tidied up the house they really ought to give it a good cleaning, neither of the boys was willing to help. Although Alan accepted the dust cloth which Anne tore from a worn-out pillow slip, the lifeless way he let it dangle from his hand and his dillydally progress across the room betrayed how little he was inclined to be helpful.

David complained that to use a broom or carpet sweeper might make his thumb swell up and hurt worse, where he had cut it yesterday. Unless he was careful it might give him blood poisoning.

"There'd be no danger of blood poison in the pasture,

I suppose," Anne remarked, taking up the broom herself.

She was tired. Yesterday had been a long day, beginning with David's breakfast before dawn. And they had
all gone to bed much later than usual because they had
had to stay up to talk about the circus. If Mrs. Malet
had been there she would have told Anne to sleep until
noon if she felt like it this morning, to catch up. But
Mrs. Malet was a hundred miles away in Indiana, and
somebody had to get up early enough to cook breakfast
for Jodie and the two boys.

"I said I suppose it wouldn't hurt your thumb to
shoot arrows in the pasture," Anne repeated, not to
leave her meaning in doubt.

The sarcasm was lost upon David. "We're not going
to play Indians today." He was plainly relieved to have
the subject changed to something not connected with
housework. "I have to show the fellows how to tie a figure of eight, the way Captain Pegleg showed me yesterday while we were resting. Do you care if I cut the end
off that extra clothesline, Anne? Nobody ever uses it,
there in the basement."

"I thought so," she said with such a sudden thrust of
the broom under Jodie's chair Jodie had no time to pull
her feet up out of the way. "Your thumb's only an ex-

cuse. You wouldn't ever have remembered about it if I hadn't asked you to help clean."

"It's not either an excuse." David denied it indignantly, gingerly loosening one end of the somewhat soiled adhesive with which the tip of his thumb was taped to show Alan and Jodie.

"Just look how red it is." He would have let Anne see his thumb too, but she was so busy sweeping under the table she did not turn her head. "What makes it so dangerous is 'cause onion juice got into it," he explained, patting the adhesive down again with as tender care as a surgeon after an operation. "If you don't believe onion juice is bad for cuts, just ask Captain Pegleg. That's the reason he paid me out of his own pocket to help him, because he says onions don't do a fellow any good, inside or out."

David had purchased his circus ticket yesterday with cash earned in the cook tent as private assistant to one of the cooks' helpers, peeling onions for stew. He had had so much to tell about Captain Pegleg last night and again this morning, how many times he had sailed the Seven Seas and rounded the Horn and how he had always been the one to go aloft to furl the sails when no one else dared, that the part Alan had taken in the parade seemed quite tame by comparison.

The only reason the Captain was now working for the

circus, David explained, was that he wished to lay up a little money so as not to be obliged to ride the rails like a hobo to New Orleans, where he intended to ship again for the Caribbean. There wasn't anything the Captain did not know about ships, David declared, and if he'd had more time he would have taught David how to splice a cable and tie a carrick bend. Unless David practiced the figure of eight this morning he might forget and not be able to do it. So would it be all right if he cut about ten feet off the extra clothesline?

Alan let fall his dust cloth to fetch the butcher knife from the pantry. "Want me to help cut, Dave? I have to know how to tie a eight myself. Show me, will you, Dave?"

Anne took the knife away from Alan. "I don't care the least bit how dull your hunting knives are." She had to speak rather loudly to make herself heard above the boys' protests. "You know better than to use this one.

"And don't do your cutting down there, either," she called after the two as they went clattering down the basement steps. "Take your junk to the back yard and don't make a mess in the basement."

"It's our basement just as much as it is yours," David answered back in the same tone of voice Dinky Smith used when he was being impudent to his mother. "We can make a mess down here if we want to."

They didn't, however. Instead they dragged the length of dusty rope up the steps, flapping it around like a lariat and whipping it up and down and not even noticing the dust they were making upon Anne's clean floor.

"All right, Miss Josephine Todd," Anne told Jodie as the child crumpled up her napkin and pushed aside her bowl of cereal to follow her brothers. "If you're the kind of little girl that would rather tag a mob of boys than help your sister, go ahead.

"No," she continued, seeing the child hesitate, uncertain whether to go or stay, "I don't want your help. I wouldn't let you if you offered." And she turned her back toward Jodie as though to make a stranger of her.

A long minute or two of uncomfortable silence, an indistinct scrabbly sound of small feet tiptoeing across the floor, a bang of the screen door, and Jodie went flying down the yard to join the boys before they reached the pasture.

It was the last straw. That the boys should not be willing to do their share of work had been disappointing enough, or perhaps not so much a disappointment as it was grounds for righteous indignation. But that Jodie should desert her, that Jodie should choose to side with David and Alan and leave Anne with the whole house to clean without anyone to aid her at all, hurt Anne's feelings.

She might even have shed a few tears except that she was so out of sorts with the boys. She had a right to be indignant, she told herself. Anyone else in her place would have given the boys a good scolding and made them stay indoors till the work was finished. Going off to play in the pasture as though it weren't as much their responsibility as hers to keep things clean now that they had no housekeeper!

The harder Anne pushed the carpet sweeper back and forth, first across the rug in the dining room and then in the living room, the greater her sense of grievance grew. What was the use of trying to behave like a mother and not letting her temper boil over when the children did something wrong? They didn't appreciate it. Why should she have to work all morning while they played in the pasture? She had as much right to have a good time as they had.

Her shoulders ached, she had a crick in her back from pushing the sweeper so long, and her eyes smarted with dust—or perhaps from the effort of holding back the hot tears. The dust cloth caught upon the base of the lamp and she barely succeeded in righting it before it toppled.

"Anyone at home?" queried a neighborly voice at the kitchen door. "My goodness sakes!" Mrs. Scott exclaimed a moment later, surveying the living room. "You're so spick-and-span clean in here it puts my house to shame."

She looked into the dining room to admire the orderliness there too. "Don't tell me you did it all yourself, Anne!"

For some unaccountable reason the praise almost made Anne burst into tears. She could not trust her voice to reply.

Fortunately Mrs. Scott seemed not to notice. "The rugs certainly never looked so clean while Mrs. Lloyd was in charge," she continued, still gazing around her. (While she was not observing, Anne dried her eyes upon the hem of her dress.) "There's many a grown person would not be so conscientious as you, child. Wait till I tell Rose Malet! She'll be mortal proud to hear what a fine housekeeper you are turning into.

"Here, let me finish the dusting while you run upstairs and wash your hands. When I saw the boys go down the yard I said to myself maybe I could persuade you to keep me company for lunch. It's too bad I didn't think about it earlier, to prepare larger quantities, to invite the others too. It's only a snack, hardly enough for the two of us."

Nor would she accept Anne's excuse that maybe she ought not come, maybe she ought to stay at home to get lunch for the children.

"A boy who can peel onions a whole morning in a circus tent is certainly competent to cut a few slices of bread and open a tin can," Mrs. Scott declared, her gentle voice quite firm. "You've done enough for one day. Now it's their turn. You mustn't spoil the boys, Anne, doing their tasks for them."

Anne would have liked to defend herself, to explain that it wasn't her fault because the boys had gone off to play at sailors in the pasture; she had tried to make them help but they wouldn't. Loyalty stayed the words from speech, however. It would not be right to blame the boys; it might give Mrs. Scott a bad opinion of them.

"Unless they learn to lend a hand in the house, how will their wives ever be able to manage?" Under her plain gray hair Mrs. Scott's eyes were twinkling. "Imagine, with babies to tend and the Sewing Circle to entertain and a husband so feckless he can't even whisk a broom!"

Anne was beginning to feel like herself again, not half so tired and abused. Indeed so ridiculous a picture flashed into her mind at Mrs. Scott's words she had to giggle— a picture of herself in long skirts dishing out refreshments right and left as fast as she could to the ladies of the Sewing Circle, with half a dozen babies just big enough to toddle grabbing at her skirts and getting under foot so she almost tripped and spilled the ice cream.

"I 'spect the wives would send Davie and Alan back home to me till I taught them better," she poked her brown head over the banister to reply as she dashed upstairs to tidy herself. "Nor I wouldn't blame the wives the least bit, either!"

Mrs. Scott was as good a cook as Mrs. Malet. In fact the two often exchanged recipes and borrowed each other's magazines to see what new gadgets were advertised to make housekeeping easy for those who had money to afford them. This noon Mrs. Scott had baked chicken hash with brown gravy to use up the left-overs, and boiled a couple of roasting ears fresh from the garden to eat piping hot, dripping with butter.

Later in the month when the corn was in more plentiful supply, she would be glad for Anne to take some from the garden for her family. "Maybe I should stipulate that it's only on condition you make the boys shuck it and remove the silks," she added jokingly. "I'm not of a mind to put you to extra work." And although Anne was aware that Mrs. Scott was only being humorous, still it seemed a very good suggestion.

Anne enjoyed the leisurely luncheon conversation as much as the food itself, though of course in a different way. Mrs. Scott was not the sort of person who asked prying questions. Nor did she think Anne ought to change her ways of doing things. As a matter of fact she complimented her upon how well she was managing.

"The trouble is," Anne didn't mind admitting, "the

main trouble is, Alan and David would rather play than do housework. They don't want to work unless it's something they like to do, such as making cookies and boiling wieners to eat with buns. Mrs. Malet used to let them sometimes."

Mrs. Scott nodded vigorously. "You've hit the nail square on the head," she agreed. "There never was a boy yet who wouldn't rather run and play. It's the nature of boys, like colts. I remember what a time I used to have with my Jack, getting him to do his chores. Sometimes I was so vexed with his tricks and shenanigans I fairly lost my mind."

It was a surprise to Anne that Mrs. Scott's son used to behave like that, because now he was such a serious sort of man, with two children of his own.

While Anne carried the plates to the kitchen Mrs. Scott dished up the applesauce and cut the gingerbread. The square she put upon Anne's plate was so thick, still warm from the oven, brown and spicy and crumbly sweet, Anne wished she had a pocket in her dress she could slip it into, to take home to the children. It could easily be divided into three smaller pieces. She had already eaten so much lunch the applesauce would be as much dessert as she needed.

"You know, Anne"—Mrs. Scott poured herself a cup of coffee—"I do believe you've not only hit the nail on the head about the nature of boys, but you have hit upon a solution for your problem.

"Letting them choose the work they prefer, I mean. And if you don't mind my making a suggestion, why not go a step farther and organize yourselves into a committee to decide in case any arguments arise? If the boys wish to take over part of the cooking, I'll be glad to give them a lesson now and then. I shouldn't be surprised if David learned to cook rather well, though I should never expect him to acquire your knack at it."

The prospect of a family committee was so attractive Anne dried the dishes for Mrs. Scott with double speed, to get home to start the committee as soon as possible. Luckily she had had experience with committees, both at school and at Sunday-school, and had been chairman of the seventh grade Library Club, so she knew how to preside and how motions are made and seconded. Of course she intended to let the children elect whomever they wished to be chairman, but she was practically positive they would all vote for her.

"You'd do me a favor to take the rest of the gingerbread home with you." Mrs. Scott was tearing off a piece of waxed paper to wrap it. "It'll grow stale if it's left here."

"Refreshments for the first Todd meeting," Anne exclaimed, then affected to be mistrustful. "You don't think it would be a risk? The boys might get the notion it's to be a social committee instead of a work one."

The children had not yet returned from the pasture, which gave Anne an opportunity to hide the gingerbread for a surprise until they had elected officers. Everybody must have an office, she realized now that she had time to plan. David could be assistant chairman and Alan secretary, to print the announcements on a sheet of paper about who was to do what. Jodie could be door-keeper, like the one Micky Moore said they had in the lodge his father belonged to, to make people give the password so no outsiders could get in.

Anne opened a can of corn to heat for the children's lunch and cut the bread and removed the butter from the refrigerator to let it soften. At the last minute while they were washing their hands she would fry an egg apiece, taking pains not to break the yolks like Mrs. Lloyd. The children did not like the yolks broken.

Her preparations were interrupted by a ring at the doorbell, a sudden sharp ring, followed by a long one. It must be an agent, with brushes to sell or magazine sub-scriptions. Everybody else would be at home having lunch at this time of day. If it were any of her or the boys' friends they wouldn't come to the front door. She dried her hands on a kitchen towel and went to see.

A man stood at the front door, a stranger, an elderly,

middle-sized man in a blue suit. His face was red because it was a hot day, and he had pushed his hat far to the back of his head to mop his forehead.

"Don't get scared, Daughter." He stuck the handkerchief into his hip pocket and lifted his hat politely. "I'm not here to make any arrests."

Not until he said *arrests* did it occur to Anne that he was a policeman. There were no policemen in Springtown because everyone was friends with everyone else, or at least they all knew each other, and nobody in Springtown was a burglar or tried to pass counterfeit money or anything like that.

"My name is Pettit, Officer Pettit, from Centerville," he introduced himself. "Mind if I come in to talk to you for a few minutes?"

Anne unlatched the screen door and invited him to have a chair by the window in the living room where there was a breeze. It was so astonishing that a policeman should wish to speak with her she didn't know what to make of it.

"This 'tarnal heat catches a man where he minds it most," he complained, easing himself with a sigh into the deep armchair. "A fellow with any gumption'd have known better than to wear new shoes. This July weather makes 'em swell up twice their size." Anne supposed it must be his feet, not the shoes, which swelled up.

He leaned forward to extract the handkerchief from his hip pocket again, to wipe the perspiration from his face before he flicked the grayish dust from the tips of his tan oxfords.

"Got off the bus a couple of miles back," he continued as if to account for the dust, "to see a man 'bout raspberries my wife wants for jelly-makin'. Had to foot it the rest of the way here. Whew, is it hot—hotter than Tophet!" He made a motion as though to dry his face again, thought better of it, and stuffed the dusty kerchief hastily into his rear pocket. "Feels cool in here, though, nice and cool.

"Your name Todd?" he inquired.

"Yes, sir, Anne Todd." Until that moment she had assumed he must have come to the wrong house, or else had stopped in to rest himself on his way somewhere else. That he had come on purpose made her feel a little odd, almost as though she were somebody else in somebody else's house.

"Any brothers and sisters?"

"Yes, sir. My brother David is ten and Alan is seven. Jodie's only five. She's a girl." Although Anne's chair was not near a window the air seemed to blow chilly against the back of her neck.

"Your pa is in furrin parts, I understand?" Perhaps Officer Pettit thought he might appear to be asking too many questions, for he added in a deprecatory manner, "No cause for you to be upset. Judge Neal sent me 'round just to make a few inquires and have a look around."

Anne did not know why Mr. Pettit should think she was upset, because she wasn't. She felt quite self-possessed, she was not the least bit excited. Of course anyone would be a little anxious when a policeman had come all the way from Centerville to ask questions, but since she had not broken the law there was no reason why she should be scared. No reason at all.

"My father will come home in a few months, as soon as he finishes building a road for the oil company. It's in Ecuador—the road is, I mean." She summoned breath to steady her voice for a query of her own. "Who's Judge Neal? And why does he want to know about us?"

"He's a judge," said Officer Pettit.

He ran a hand across the top of his head and absently adjusted the ends of his blue bow-tie as if trying to make up his mind how much to go into detail. "I don't know as I ought to tell you— Still an' all, I don't know why I oughtn't, neither."

He glanced to right and left to make certain they were alone. "Somebody sent the judge a complaint," he informed her in a tone too low to be overheard by any possible eavesdropper who might be lurking in the next room. "Sent it through the mail. I can't say what was the contents of it exactly, not readin' it myself, but it come yestiddy. From Dover, it was. I just happened to look at the postmark when I was emptyin' out the wastebasket for the judge.

"Now don't you go frettin' yourself. When I turn in

my report that'll most likely be the end of it. I don't see why someone 'way 'cross county in Dover should be writin' about somebody in Springtown, anyhow. Prob'ly some old crank wantin' to stir up trouble.

"No sirree, don't you trouble your little head about it. When I report how neat you keep the house, and how mannerly you behave yourself, that ought to make an end on it. Your brothers don't happen to be here, so I could have a look at them?" he questioned as an afterthought.

"They're not in the house right now, sir."

Despite the heavy sensation in the pit of her stomach as though a sharp rock had lodged there, Anne's mind worked quickly. It would never do to let the policeman see Davie and Alan when they first came from the pasture, wearing their oldest overalls and looking like ragamuffins with their hair not combed and most likely muddied from head to foot. If boys are dirty, people believe they are bad boys.

"Could you come back this afternoon, about two or three o'clock? They'll be here by that time." The instant they came into the house she would send them upstairs to take a bath and change into their best clothes, before they ate lunch.

Mr. Pettit reached for his hat upon the library table where he had deposited it beside a bowl of yellow nasturtiums. "Been gone too long already." He consulted his watch and shook his head. "Stoppin' off to see about those raspberries took longer than I allowed.

"How old did you say the boys are—seven and ten? At that age they can't be of a size to do much damage. That's what I'll tell the judge."

Anne was in such a hurry to have him depart before the boys appeared that her hand shook as she poured him a glass of cold water from the refrigerator jar, at his request for a drink. Before she carried the tumbler into the living room she took a hasty glance out the back window. To her relief the children were not in sight.

Officer Pettit drank the water almost at one gulp. "I've got to get a move on if I'm goin' to catch the one-thirty bus. It's two hours till the next one.

"Thanks for the drink." He handed her the tumbler and plopped his hat upon his head and extended a hand in hasty farewell. "So long."

And he was gone.

6

A BUS TRIP

Anne's first impulse was to find out from Mrs. Scott whether she thought a visit from a policeman was a very serious matter and what Anne should do about it.

Although Mrs. Scott had never expressed an opinion of Mrs. Lloyd, Anne had reason to believe she did not hold her in high regard. The two of them never used to have a cup of coffee together in the middle of the morning like Mrs. Malet and Mrs. Scott, nor did they ever sit upon each other's porch to sew in the afternoon. And once when Anne had mentioned the new silk dress Mrs. Scott had worn to church, Mrs. Lloyd had pulled down the corners of her mouth and said, "That woman, it's nothing to me what she wears."

So it would not be like criticizing one of Mrs. Scott's particular friends to tell her about the letter Mrs. Lloyd had written to the judge, and to ask her honest opinion whether she didn't think it was wrong of Mrs. Lloyd. Not only wrong, but really mean and spiteful!

For it must have been Mrs. Lloyd who had sent the complaint. It couldn't have been anyone else, especially since she was the only person who lived in Dover, at least the only person with whom Anne was acquainted.

People who lived in Springtown would not do a thing like that; they were nice and friendly. They would not send a policeman even when boys happened to break a window playing ball or stole some apples from their trees, which neither David nor Alan ever did anyhow. They kept to their own yard to play or went to the pasture, where they had a right to do as they pleased because Father had bought the pasture when he bought the house.

Mrs. Lloyd knew as well as anybody that Davie and Alan were not bad boys, and she had no right to say they were. They might sometimes shirk doing their work and they didn't always behave themselves, but they told the truth and when they promised to do something they could be depended upon to do it. It was not fair of Mrs. Lloyd to give them a bad reputation, with no chance to defend themselves. . . . For a few minutes after Officer

Pettit's departure Anne was too indignant to feel apprehensive about possible further consequences.

"Hi, Anne, where are you?" the boys called out, pounding like wild ponies into the kitchen. "Anything to eat? Boy, am I hungry!"

"Boy, am I hungwy!" Jodie panted after them, out of breath from trying to keep up in the race from the pasture.

Although there was no reason why the family should feel humiliated by Mr. Pettit's visit, Anne decided not to let the children know about it, at least not just yet. They were so young they might get excited and tell the neighbors, and she did not approve of airing family affairs in public.

In her concern to appear natural, as though nothing unusual had happened, she forgot the gingerbread. If Alan had not smelled it when he went into the pantry to set the pans away, it might have remained upon the shelf until it grew stale.

"It's refreshments for a committee meeting this afternoon," she told him, replacing the cover. "There's only enough to go 'round to the members."

"Maybe somebody won't come," Alan suggested hopefully. "Whyn't we eat her piece right now? Or maybe two people won't come and we can have both of theirs." He wiped his mouth with the back of his hand in anticipation. "Let's eat their pieces now, Anne, 'fore anyone gets here."

"No," she replied, shaking her head, so sober and quiet they all believed she must be in earnest. "They will all want their share, and every single member will be here." The memory of the policeman kept getting into the way of the fun she had expected the family committee to be.

She made an effort to put some excitement into her voice and gave two brisk taps with the fork she was putting away, as though to call a meeting to order. "In fact, all the members are already here inside the house."

"I don't see anyone," Jodie said blankly, turning around to look. "Nobody 'cept just us."

"I do," David announced, suddenly catching on, his eyes bright with satisfaction to be the first to guess. "I see one, two, three people and me— That makes four people. It's us, isn't it, Anne?"

"It's to be a work committee," she warned them solemnly, "hard work with a capital W," but the warning only whetted their eagerness. "No one needs to join who doesn't wish to.

"It's the Todd Committee to look after the family and manage till Mrs. Malet comes back. Everyone who wishes to become a member please signify by raising your right hand."

Upon the instant three hands shot up into the air, three voices clamored in mixed chorus, "I want to! Me too, me too! So do I!"

The children's enthusiasm set spark to her own. "The first item on the agenda"—it was a word Anne had learned when she was elected chairman of the seventh grade Library Club—"is the election of officers. But first we must serve the refreshments.

"David, will you please cut the gingerbread into three equal pieces? I've already had my share, over at Mrs. Scott's."

The zeal of the committee reached such a high pitch it was voted to sweep and dust the upstairs right away, and whoever wished to cook supper and wash dishes should be allowed to. Although Anne had had more than enough of house-cleaning for the time being and would have preferred to go downtown to the library to get a book to read, she voted with the others in order to make it unanimous. Besides, the thought occurred to her—for even while she presided over the meeting and counted votes she could not get the policeman out of her mind— Officer Pettit might take it into his head to pay another surprise visit tomorrow to inspect their housekeeping.

It was not until she was in bed and the house was quiet and dark that she was able to give uninterrupted thought to what misdoings Mrs. Lloyd might have reported to the judge. . . . David would probably have to accept responsibility for the Incas' attack upon the clothesline, since he was leader of the gang. Still, it was not as though the underwear had been torn or damaged. Mud would come out in the wash, it didn't stain like paint or tar. A little soap and warm water would be sufficient.

As for Alan, the only bad thing he had done recently was to behave like a locomotive and run chug-chug at Mrs. Lloyd to scare her. But he was so small and she was so big he could not have injured her even if he had run smack against her. And anyhow she had hopped out of the way so fast he had not touched her.

In spite of Anne's attempts to persuade herself that Mrs. Lloyd had very little to complain about, and in spite of her quoting to herself Mr. Pettit's statement that when he turned in his report that would most likely be the end of it all, she could not help becoming more and more uneasy.

During the daytime worrisome thoughts can be pushed out of sight behind other thoughts and sometimes they can be quite forgotten. But when you are lying awake in the dark with nobody to turn to in your trouble and you know that you are responsible for the safety of your brothers and your baby sister, the worry and the responsibility together increase to unmanageable proportions.

. . . What if the judge should send Davie and Alan to a reform school? Maybe that was what Mrs. Lloyd had told him to do.

If only there had been an opportunity to discuss matters with Mrs. Scott! It might not be too late yet. She often stayed up until eleven o'clock to read or listen to the radio.

But when Anne slid out of bed to tiptoe across to the hall window, the cottage next door stood dark as a shadow in the white moonshine. It must be ever so much later than she had realized, perhaps midnight, with everything so hushed and unmoving, not even a dog barking in the distance nor the wind stirring in the apple tree under the window—as if the moon had laid a spell upon the earth and she alone remained alive to look and listen.

Perhaps it was the chill of the floor under her bare feet which made her shiver, or it may have been lonesomeness or discouragement. She felt like writing to her father to come home, not to wait until he had earned enough money to send them to college. Only there was no stationery upstairs and if she should turn on the light the children might waken.

When the monthly check came from the oil company maybe they might pack a suitcase and go to Indiana to stay with Mrs. Malet until her daughter got well and

Mrs. Malet could come home. There ought to be plenty of room for them on Mrs. Malet's daughter's farm, and if there wasn't, the children could sleep double. They would all help with the work to pay for the groceries they ate. . . . With which comforting thought Anne at last feel asleep.

It was so late when the household awakened the next morning that when Anne went to the door to fetch in the bottles of milk for breakfast she saw Mrs. Scott leaving the house. She must be intending to spend the day in Sandtown with her son and his family, or perhaps two or three days, since she was carrying a satchel.

Of a sudden, as when the gates of a dam give way to let the waters come rushing through, the cares which had beset Anne's night came flooding back to trouble the sunlit morning. She had counted upon Mrs. Scott to stand up for her and the boys in case they needed it. Now that she would be away, there was no one to whom Anne could turn. Although the other neighbors were friendly, they were not particular friends like Mrs. Scott.

What if the judge should be on Mrs. Lloyd's side? What if he should say that Anne had had no right to discharge her?

Before breakfast was finished Anne had made up her mind. She and David must present their side of the case to the judge, because how otherwise would he know to give justice? Unless they stood up for themselves and explained exactly what had happened he might believe that all the right was on the housekeeper's side. If there was sufficient money in the piggy banks to buy a half-fare ticket for Alan he could go too, to speak for himself. Jodie of course could ride free, being under age.

"Davie, you and Alan hurry up and finish drinking your milk and then pry the money out of the pigs. You too, Jodie, if there's any in yours. We need every penny. There's a nail file on my dressing table you can use, and another in the bathroom. Be quick as you can, because we must get dressed up to go to Centerville."

To Anne's surprise she was beginning to be rather more cheerful, or at least much more confident, as though with her decision to go to the judge half the battle had already been won.

"Did someone invite us?" David lingered to inquire. "Is it a picnic, Anne?"

It was a business matter, she told him, something serious which she could not discuss now, since they must catch the eleven o'clock bus, but she would explain later. Because he was a boy and next oldest she was depending upon him to help her. She was certain the two of them together would be able to set things right.

"Get a move on yourself, Al," she heard him issuing commands with big-brotherly authority a minute or two

later. "I and Anne must 'tend to important business in Centerville, and it's up to you whether you go along or get left behind. You too, Jodie."

A boy like Davie was a real comfort to have in the family, Anne thought to herself. If he were as scatter-brained and spoiled as Dinky Smith, she didn't know how she could ever manage.

Anne sat with David on the bus, with Jodie and Alan across the aisle where she could keep an eye on them, each with a seat by the window. There were so few passengers the driver declared he ought to charge double, but even Jodie knew he did not mean it.

It is less pleasurable to travel upon a bus which is practically empty. Anne missed the flurry and lively

bustle of people getting on and off, lugging curiously shaped bundles which must contain something unusual if there were any way of finding out what. And sometimes on a crowded bus there is a passenger who looks so odd and mysterious he is almost bound to be a detective or a miser or maybe someone in disguise the authorities would be willing to pay a reward for. Still, as Anne told David, it was better for them that the bus was not crowded. They could talk as much as they wished about the business which was taking them to Centerville, with nobody to overhear them.

As a matter of fact, however, after the first few minutes neither of them had much to say. It is possible that David was regretting the part he had taken in the attack upon the clothesline, or that he was pondering the kind of punishment which might be meted out to him, but Anne did not think so. His chief concern seemed to be the fast freight train which steamed and puffed alongside the bus on the tracks parallel to the highway, with a new red-painted caboose attached at the end. The caboose sometimes gained upon the bus, sometimes lost ground, depending upon how much the driver stepped up speed.

Anne noticed that Alan now occupied the seat directly behind the driver, occasionally leaning forward to ask a question—probably about what would happen if the clutch slipped, or whether a locomotive or a bus was easier to run. Since the driver seemed not to object to being talked to, Anne saw no reason for her objecting either. The *Do-Not-Talk-to-the-Driver* sign probably did not apply except at times when the driver was not in a mood to answer.

As for Anne herself, a trip to Centerville was not so commonplace an event she could afford to miss any of the sights to be seen along the way. Having no particular interest in the freight train, she moved across the aisle to have a window to herself behind Jodie. It was enjoyable to watch the fields slide past, green of waving corn, greenish gold of ripening wheat, with the sky so blue and the sun so hot the air shimmered like water.

Colts in a pasture tossed their heads and kicked up their heels and ran to their mothers, pretending to be afraid of the bus, and black and white pigs wallowed in a muddy pond to cool themselves off. Anne would have liked to look longer at the pigs. They always had such shrewd little eyes and grunted so knowingly she was sure they must have their own opinion of people just as people had their own opinion of pigs.

Maple trees marched in leafy procession up to the front doors of farmhouses, wide-branched oaks and elms stood single in meadows to make spots of shade for the cows, and in a dried-up creek bed under a clump of sycamores three little girls with their skirts rolled up about their waists were wading in a pool the creek had left behind.

Once or twice as the bus slowed down to skirt a cluster of houses at a crossroads Anne caught a whiff of dinners cooking—fried ham and hot apple pie and bread that somebody must be baking. Even the boiled cabbage, which was not one of her favorite vegetables, smelled so good it made her hungry.

"Jugtown," the driver called out, bringing the bus to a stop. "Jugtown on the Pike. Ten minute stop for refreshments, restaurant at the right."

But he was the only one who got off. When he returned a few minutes later he was carrying a bottle of strawberry pop with two straws, one for himself and one for Alan. It almost made Anne wish she were a boy, and small like Alan. When you are as old as Anne people think you are too big to offer refreshments to unless you are acquainted. And of course you really are.

Now they were under way again, the breeze cooling Anne's cheeks and fanning her hair. It would not be long until they were in Centerville. They had already crossed the river on the outskirts, shrunken by the spell of dry weather until it was hardly larger than the creek in the pasture at home.

Anne wished she were going on and on, as far as the bus went and farther. It was fun to travel. Maybe that is what she would do when she was grown—be a traveler and see the world instead of having children and a husband to cook and keep house for. Not the kind of traveler who sells brushes or fancy lace tablecloths, but one who rides in planes and Pullman cars and crosses the ocean in a ship. There were so many things she longed to behold with her own eyes—mountains and a glacier, the ocean and a canal, Niagara Falls and a volcano, a kingdom with a king and queen and beautiful princesses—

"Centerville! All passengers for Centerville dismount here!" bawled the driver, drawing up to the curbstone at the bus station. "Don't forget your packages, ladies.

" 'Fore you know it, your little brother'll be sitting at

the wheel of a bus himself," the driver told Anne, grinning at her over Alan's head as she came up the aisle with Jodie. "He's got the hang of it now, no mistake.

"So long, Al. If ever I have a layover in Springtown I'll look you up."

Alan waved good-bye from the sidewalk. "So long, Pete." He was so proud to be hailed as an equal by the driver that he strutted like a bantam rooster as the four of them set off down the maple-shaded street toward the Square and the courthouse.

7

THE JUDGE

The courthouse stood in the middle of the Square, an old-fashioned, three-storied structure of yellowish brick and gray stone, surrounded by a somewhat frayed and dusty lawn. Fronting upon it on all four sides were shops and stores and restaurants, a bank or two and a barber shop—a collection almost large enough for a city, with far more to attract the eye than in straggling Springtown.

Except for two or three dogs drowsing under parked cars, Anne and the children had the Square to themselves, perhaps because it was so nearly noon, or perhaps because the sun struck so hot upon cement sidewalks and brick walls and pavements that everyone preferred to remain indoors in the shade. The children would have enjoyed lingering to look into the windows, and indeed there was much to see. The two boys were especially interested in the array of fishing rods and bicycles and Boy Scout knives and cooking kits on display behind the plate glass of the hardware store, but unless they hurried, Anne warned David, it might be too late to see the judge.

If she had been alone she might well have been tempted to put off the visit to the judge until some other time, the courthouse looked so forbidding. It was odd that she had never happened to notice before what a stand-offish, unfriendly appearance it had, but then she had never before had any reason to pay attention to it. The blinds were drawn against the sun, the door gaping open, with not a single soul in sight except a man lounging against the side of the courthouse with his hat pulled down to shade his face.

"You must keep quiet in the courthouse, like church," Anne cautioned the two younger children to keep them from asking questions. "Davie and I have to talk to a judge."

If only today were tomorrow and the ordeal were over with! Or if only it were still yesterday! If she had it to do over again, she would wait until next week when Mrs. Scott could accompany them. Mrs. Scott would have known how to talk to an important person like a judge, and he would have paid more attention to what she said.

Well, it was no use wishing for Mrs. Scott. Now that they had spent their money to get here, they would just have to stand up for themselves. "If you haven't spunk enough to stand up for yourself," Anne reminded herself sternly, "you've no right to expect someone else to do it for you. And anyhow the judge isn't a bear, he's not going to eat you." But the reminder did not make her feel particularly bolder.

"You'll be good, Alan, won't you?" she said, not so much to admonish him as to take her mind off herself. "Show people how well boys from Springtown can behave."

At the sound of her voice the man leaning against the courthouse wall roused from his nap to push back his hat to see who was speaking. Or perhaps he was already awake and only waiting for something to happen which might require his attention.

"Bless my soul," he exclaimed, opening his eyes wide to stare at her and taking out his handkerchief to mop his brow. "Why, bless my soul if it ain't the same little girl I talked to yestiddy in Springtown!"

It was Mr. Pettit, Officer Pettit himself, and he seemed so pleased to see Anne she could not help feeling rather flattered. "We came on the eleven o'clock bus," she explained. "I thought we'd better not put it off.

"David, this is Mr. Pettit that I was telling you about," she introduced them to each other.

"Shake hands with Mr. Pettit, Alan. Mr. Pettit is a policeman friend of mine." It was not everybody, she was just beginning to realize with a pleasurable sense of satisfaction, in fact it was hardly anybody who was lucky enough to be friends with a policeman. Not Jennie Allen, for instance, nor even Micky Moore, for that matter. She doubted whether either of them was well enough acquainted with a police officer to have him speak to them on the street.

"Don't hang back, Jodie. Give Mr. Pettit your hand. He likes little girls."

"Come right in," said Officer Pettit. Had it been his own house he was inviting them into, he could scarcely have been more hospitable. "Walk right in, the whole kit and caboodle of you!" He motioned them to precede him into the darkened foyer where a white-faced clock ticked sluggishly, high upon the wall.

"Thought you'd take matters into your own hands and answer the complaint in person, did you?" he inquired, taking out his red-checked handkerchief again to dust the bench beneath the clock for the children to seat themselves. "Likely it's the best policy. Proves you've not done anything you're not willing to face up to.

"You'd be surprised," he remarked in an aside to Anne, "how many folks is not willing to face up when it comes to consequences. Grown folks. Yes, you'd be surprised."

"Yes, sir," she replied. It was gratifying to have him address her as one grown-up to another, as though she might be the children's parent. And the fact that he approved of their coming made her feel more confident.

"Make yourselves comfortable while I go upstairs to tell Judge Neal's stenographer. Court is not in session this week, but there's always plenty to keep him busy. Partly on 'count of extra work he's put to by cranks wanting to invoke the law for one fool thing or 'nother.

"Not to mention 'bout a letter you and me heard about that one of the crack-brains wrote, eh, young lady?" Over the children's heads Officer Pettit winked broadly at Anne. "Some folks ain't got anything better to do than try to make trouble, but they're 'bout to get their come-uppance, ain't that so, Miss Anne?"

His manner was so waggish, he affected such an air of mock severity, like a boy playing at being grown up, she could not help laughing.

"I can't say about that," she told him, "but Mrs. Lloyd is certainly plenty cranky, if that's what you mean."

Which saucy remark, although it would undoubtedly have stirred the former housekeeper's wrath to hear, for some unaccountable reason seemed to act like a tonic upon Anne's own spirits, almost to the point of making her reckless.

Who did Mrs. Lloyd think she was that she should attempt to scare them, threatening to make them "rue the day"? She had no power over them, she was just an ordinary person, not different from other people except that she was cross and crabby and didn't like children. And when the judge asked, Anne would not be afraid to tell him that Mrs. Lloyd only wanted to get even because she had been discharged. Though of course David would still have to be responsible for what he and his tribe of Indians had done to the clothesline.

Anne borrowed David's pocket comb to arrange Jodie's curls, wind-blown from the bus ride, and ran it through her own straight brown locks to make herself look presentable.

Jodie was thirsty, and while she quenched her thirst at the drinking fountain outside the entrance Anne wet a corner of her handkerchief to wipe the dust from her warm little fingers. People must not get the impression that Anne neglected to keep the children clean, now that they were without a housekeeper. Though, if the

truth were known, there were times when no amount of persuasion or exhortation—even from Mrs. Malet—could prevail upon either of the boys to take a bath. It was fortunate that the committee had voted last evening in favor of the tub and soap.

The minutes at the drinking fountain must have sped faster than Anne was aware, for Officer Pettit appeared to summon her and Jodie. The judge would see them immediately, he informed her; the two boys had already gone up to his sanctum. What a sanctum was, Anne did not know, but it did not sound very pleasant. Maybe it was a special kind of office with iron bars like a jail.

It was a long climb up the two flights of twisting stairs for legs as short as Jodie's, but she made what speed she could, pulling herself up by the rungs of the banister. She seemed to sense the uneasiness which made Anne so subdued. At the top of the second flight Officer Pettit motioned them toward a high-ceilinged, green-painted room where the sun struck through in thin shafts of light around the edges of the drawn shades.

David and Alan were already seated in wide-armed chairs in front of the judge's roll-top desk. A tall, soldierly man with gray hair, the judge had swung his swivel chair around to face the boys, his back toward the door.

Anne and Jodie stepped on tiptoe across the doorsill to wait until he should take notice of them.

He was speaking to Alan. "Your sister looks after the family, you say." The voice was deep, the words quiet and clear—not shapeless-sounding and all-run-together like Mr. Pettit's sentences. "She's quite a big girl, no doubt, old enough to be in high school?"

Alan shook his head. "She doesn't go to high school. She goes to the same one Dave and I go to, on Hazel Street. Micky Moore's sister goes to high school."

He slid forward in his chair to let his feet dangle nearer the floor, swinging them thoughtfully back and forth while he deliberated what answer to make to the other half of the question. Having always taken Anne's size for granted, he had never given it any thought.

"She's not great big, Anne isn't," he concluded after a moment's pause, bringing his feet to rest upon a rung of the chair. "She's only sort of bigity."

The word Alan had chosen to describe her so embarrassed Anne that she longed to slip out of sight and down the stairs before the judge caught sight of her. Of course Alan had not intended to give a bad impression of her. He thought the word meant "medium big." But the judge would not know that, and she could not explain. He would believe that she was conceited and gave herself airs and acted as though she thought she was superior to other people. Especially as it was her very own brother who had said it. . . . She had faults—she was willing to admit that she wasn't perfect, she lost her temper and couldn't remember to be patient until afterward when it was too late—but nobody had ever accused her of being stuck-up and bigity. Because she wasn't, she honestly wasn't!

"We're here, Judge," Officer Pettit announced, hat in hand. "Here's the boys' big sister from Springtown, like I said, come to see 'bout that complaint from Dover.

"Little Curly-top's their sister too, ain't that so, Curly?" He winked at Jodie, who turned her head away, not altogether displeased to have him seek her favor, but self-conscious and shy.

"Anne Todd, meet his honor, Judge Neal." Mr. Pettit pronounced it *jedge*. "Now, sir, if I'm not needed, I'd best be gettin' back to my patrol duties."

"Thank you, Pettit."

As courteous as though she were a lady grown, Judge Neal rose to extend his hand in getting. "So this is Bigity Anne!"

Ill at ease though she was, her face still burning with mortification that Alan should have given her so poor a reputation, she was aware even through the fog of her embarrassment that Judge Neal was smiling. With a sudden sense of relief, so sharp she could feel it in the pit of her stomach like an over-hasty swallow of cold water, she realized that he must not have taken Alan seriously. Being a judge, he must have known that Alan had used the wrong word. The thought was like a cool breeze fanning her flushed cheeks, restoring her self-respect.

"It is a pleasure to make your acquaintance, Anne." She could tell that he meant it; he was not just saying it to be polite.

"Thank you, sir, I'm pleased to meet you, sir. Jodie, shake hands with Judge Neal. Her real name's Josephine," she explained as they settled themselves in the chairs he pulled forward, "but it's too long for her while she's still so little."

Anne enjoyed making new friends. It was not often that she had the opportunity, since she was already well acquainted with everyone who lived in Springtown. That is, with everyone of her own age. . . . When you think of your friends you don't usually count older people in, because they almost always have each other for company unless they happen to be a neighbor like Mrs. Scott or else your teacher or the parents of your particular friends —Jennie Allen's father and mother, for example, or Micky Moore's. But there was something about Judge Neal which made him seem different from other grown people, something which as soon as he spoke made you wish to count him in.

What that something was, Anne could not have told if she tried. It may have been some power in him of cheerful kindliness, or perhaps a bond she sensed between them of honesty and courage. Whatever it was, it made her feel taller and more capable, and ever so glad that she was her own self and not anyone else.

If she were a school teacher or the president of the Ladies' Aid he couldn't act more polite to her, she thought, reaching across to pull down Jodie's short pink skirts to conceal the black smudge the child had somehow managed to get on her knee. She was glad they had dressed up to come, Judge Neal was such a nice-looking man and his gray suit was so spick-and-span. Yet he was as neighborly as though he lived next door in Springtown and were not a judge at all.

"Hello, Anne." David greeted her as though they had not seen each other today. "I didn't say anything yet about the poisoned arrows. Must I tell him now or wait till he asks?"

"That is for Judge Neal to decide, Davie." She hoped the judge would not think David was failing to show him proper respect, asking her opinion first. "Most likely he hasn't got around to asking about the arrows.

"I s'pose you know why we came to see you, Judge

Neal?" she inquired politely. "It's on account of the complaint Mr. Pettit told me about. We thought you might want us to explain."

While they waited for the secretary to fetch Mrs. Lloyd's letter from the file in the inner office, David told about the gang of boys who played Incas in the pasture, and that he was chief. Only now they might decide to be sailors for a while because Captain Pegleg had taught him to tie a real sailor's knot.

"Incas?" Judge Neal seemed surprised. "Why not Cherokees or Navahos?"

"Because where my father is there's lots of Incas, so I know all about them. My father's an engineer"—David sat up tall as he could with pride—"and that's what I'm going to be too, an engineer and build bridges right out in the middle of the jungle."

"I'm not," Alan mumbled to himself, stretching forward to tie his shoe. "I'm going to be a animal trainer in a circus." But nobody heard him except Anne, and she was thinking about the letter which the secretary had laid upon the desk.

Anne watched as the judge read the letter. It was a large sheet of paper ruled with brownish lines, written in pencil on both sides, a page which might have been torn from the back of Anne's own composition book. She wished she knew what it said. It must be bad indeed to make the judge draw his brows together in a frown, his eyes grow narrow, an unsmiling blue.

Maybe the letter said such bad things about them he would not believe her and David. Maybe he would take Mrs. Lloyd's word about what they had done and think they were making up explanations to win a good opinion of themselves. The very thought brought with it a sense of guilt. Anne's face flushed, her throat grew dry.

"Your housekeeper seems to think she has been mistreated. She complains that the older boy"—Judge Neal looked at David, who squared his shoulders and lifted his chin in a valiant attempt to appear self-possessed and calm under the gravely inquiring glance—"that the older boy influenced the other boys in the neighborhood to throw mud upon her possessions. Only the fact that she returned unexpectedly, Mrs. Lloyd writes, prevented the boys from destroying her property."

"She's not our real housekeeper." Having an orderly mind, David had to make sure that that point was clearly understood before he could proceed farther. "Mrs. Lloyd was only substituting until Mrs. Malet comes back."

"Is it true that you took advantage of Mrs. Lloyd's absence to throw mud?"

"No, sir, we didn't." David cleared his throat. "We didn't know she wasn't there. We didn't even remember about her." His eyes sought Anne's.

"Go ahead, Davie," she encouraged him. "And speak up loud so you can be heard."

He cleared his throat a second time. "But we did throw mud. And I was the leader." He looked the judge straight in the eyes and spoke in a breathless kind of voice as though it were a piece he was reciting at school, hurrying to have done with it as soon as possible. "The other boys did what I said because I'm their chief when we play Indians."

Confession made and responsibility acknowledged, David relaxed his grip upon the arms of the chair and leaned back more or less at ease to await the next question. Now that he had made a clean breast of it, he could be his natural self again. And he could tell from Anne's look that she was satisfied with him.

"I am interested to hear the reason for throwing the mud." Judge Neal scanned the letter again. "Mrs. Lloyd does not say which of her possessions were damaged. Would you be willing to go into detail, David?"

Sociable by nature, David was not merely willing, he was eager to oblige. Indeed when a person like Judge Neal listens with such marked respect to what you have to say, it is a pleasure to talk. "And when we got to the back yard," David concluded his description of the Indian foray, "we were going to shoot at the fence posts.

"But then I happened to notice the clothesline and it

looked so much like the enemy with legs and skirts and things that I sort of believed it was, so I told the fellows to fire." He paused for breath, savoring again in memory the thrill of danger, the excitement of battle.

"I see," the judge commented with a thoughtful nod. "But what I still do not understand is the mud which the housekeeper speaks of."

"Poison," said David tersely, surprised that so sensible a man should fail to grasp so obvious a fact. "Mud was what we poisoned our arrows with."

Anne was amazed to see a smile flit over the judge's face. It was so quick a smile, and so quickly gone, that no one noticed it except her. Had it not been for traces of it which lingered in his eyes, she would not have believed it herself.

Before there was time even to wonder what David could have said that made Judge Neal want to laugh, she herself almost giggled out loud. For it suddenly struck her how comical the little boys had looked—dashing madly at the windy clothesline, yelling like wild Indians and shooting helter-skelter at the long-legged woolen underwear with their homemade, alder-bush arrows. She must be careful not to let David suspect that she thought it was funny, though; it might hurt his feelings.

Judge Neal put a few more questions to David, mostly about how much mud had stuck to the clothes and whether the arrows had torn any holes in the cloth and what did David think he ought to do about it?

David said he didn't know. If the judge thought he ought to, he might send Mrs. Lloyd fifty cents of the money he was saving to buy a holster. Didn't Judge Neal think fifty cents would be plenty? Because lots of the arrows didn't hit; only the best shooters knew how to take good aim. But Mrs. Lloyd would have to wait until next week for the money because they had used up all but ten cents of his savings to come to Centerville. And they couldn't take it out of the grocery money because she had taken it with her to get even with them for discharging her.

"David doesn't mean that she stole it." Anne felt it was only fair to Mrs. Lloyd to explain. "She said in the note she wrote that when you discharge somebody you have to give a month's notice, and the money was due her in advance. I s'pose it's the law."

Judge Neal's gaze traveled from Anne to David, and back to Anne again. David's face was flushed, he was breathing hard, and tears were beginning to mist his brown eyes. Not that he was particularly repentant on Mrs. Lloyd's account, but it was a blow to his boyish pride to have a man he already liked as much as he liked Judge Neal believe he was worse than other boys. Moreover it would take two or three weeks to earn the half dollar he was going to have to give Mrs. Lloyd. And unless he could buy the leather holster soon, the mail order house might be all sold out of them, and then he'd never in his whole life be able to have one, never!

Judge Neal pretended not to see the tears. "If you are willing to stand surety for your brother," he told Anne, "and if David will give me his word of honor not to make targets of any more clotheslines, I think we'll call the case closed. Can I trust you, David?"

David nodded, his throat too lumpy to permit speech.

"Nor do I believe that a cash indemnity is indicated by the evidence," the judge added in a solemn court tone, half closing his eyes as though the evidence were passing in review inside his mind, as perhaps it was. "It is my considered judgment that the damage was not of sufficient extent to warrant the imposition of a fine."

Rising from his chair, he shook hands all round, first with David because it had been he who had been on trial, and then with Anne because she was the oldest, and last of all with Alan and Jodie, who had slid hastily to the floor to stand like the others.

"I'm hungry," Alan announced, stretching his arms and twisting his neck to rest himself from sitting still, "I've not had anything to eat since breakfast."

"You describe my own situation exactly, young man." Judge Neal smiled and looked at his watch. "And I must

be considerably hungrier than you because I am considerably larger." The joke made Anne giggle, but Alan was
unaware that it was a joke. "What do you say to having
lunch with me at the Campus De Luxe across the street?"

Anne was embarrassed lest he might think he had to
invite them on account of Alan's remark. They were
much obliged, she replied, but they couldn't today; they
had already been gone from home so long they really
should be starting back on the next bus.

Judge Neal protested against so hasty a departure,
"just as we are beginning to enjoy ourselves," as he
phrased it. "You would be doing me a great favor to let
me share your company during the lunch hour. My
wife is dining with friends, and now you would doom
me to solitude!" Although his manner was mock serious,
Anne could see that he hoped they would not refuse.

"I'll go to the Campus Ducks with you." *De luxe* was
a new word to Alan, whose ear had translated it into
something more familiar. "I'd like to eat at a restaurant.
Springtown hasn't any restaurant 'cept only some stools
in front of a counter at the bus station. Nor they don't
cook anything there except coffee."

"That settles it," Judge Neal declared, taking Jodie by
the hand and Anne by the elbow and shepherding the
others ahead of them out of the office and down the

stairs. "If the county seat can't surpass the Springtown restaurant it doesn't deserve to be the county seat."

Fortunately the Campus De Luxe had but few customers and neither of the tables which stood next to the front window was occupied. The children chose the first one as offering perhaps a wider view of the Square, since the awning did not come so low at that end. Judge Neal volunteered to take the chair which put his back to the window, having had, as he said, more opportunity than his guests to observe the scene.

"I wish somebody I know would come by so they'd see me eating in a restaurant," Alan remarked, planting himself at the left of his host where he could look in both directions. "I'll bet a million dollars Dinky Smith's never had a place in the window like this. I'll bet when Dinky ate in a restaurant he had to sit 'way back where he couldn't see out, don't you, Dave?"

At the judge's request the waitress supplied not just one menu, but enough for each to have one. Even Jodie studied hers though she had not yet learned to read and could make out only a few scattered letters. Had the words been printed instead of written she could have told the names of all the letters and even a few words, such as *the* and *a* and *ice cream*. Alan required assistance with many of the words, and David and Anne too were both somewhat at a loss partly because the writing was not very plain and the ink was pale and watery, but mostly because they were not used to restaurant menus and there were so many things from which to choose.

Alan elected to have hamburgers and cherry ice cream, but David declared not for him! They could have hamburgers at home because all you had to do was put them in a pan and fry them. He wanted something extra special that you couldn't get except at a restaurant. Which sounded so logical that Alan decided to reconsider his order.

In the end, upon Judge Neal's recommendation, they all ordered fried chicken—drumsticks for the boys and Jodie, wishbones for Anne and the judge—with mashed potatoes and gravy and corn on the cob, and cherry ice cream to follow. Fried chicken had been Anne's choice all along, but she had intended to order veal loaf instead, since it cost thirty-five cents less and she did not wish to put the judge to so much expense. But when he said he voted for chicken and if they were wise they would follow his example, it would have been impolite not to.

When the waitress brought the plates there were other things besides, so many side dishes it looked like a banquet—cole slaw and hot biscuits and butter and a red-colored jam which was either strawberry or raspberry, Anne could not be sure which; mustard pickles and a

salad of lettuce and cottage cheese, with a choice of tea
or coffee or milk to drink. Everyone took milk except the
judge, who said coffee was a bad habit he couldn't break
himself of.

"Gee, am I glad we don't have to wash all these
dishes," Alan congratulated himself, watching the waitress stack the plates upon a tray to make room for dessert
dishes. "The committee wouldn't ever have any chance
to play."

They had to explain to Judge Neal about the family
committee. It was a new idea to him, and one of which
he most heartily approved. That was one of the nice
things about him, Anne thought, he wasn't a bit nosey,
yet he was interested in how they managed the housekeeping and where the money came from to pay for the
groceries and whether they wouldn't rather have a grown
person staying in the house.

"We don't need one," she told him, "at least not until
Mrs. Malet gets back. Mrs. Scott is going to show the
boys how to cook, and anything we don't know we can
ask her. She lives next door to us."

"Mrs. Lloyd referred in her letter to the number of
months since you had received word from your father.
Are you expecting him to return soon?"

There was something in Judge Neal's voice—the carefully casual tone, as though he did not wish her to be-

lieve that the question was important—or perhaps it was no more than the mention of Mrs. Lloyd, which made Anne's throat go tight and dry. For a moment, only a moment, it was as if some danger threatened, vague and menacing as in a bad dream.

"As soon as the road he's building is finished he is coming home." She swallowed to loosen her throat. "It was supposed to be finished next September, but it may take a little longer.

"The reason we haven't been getting his letters is because he has to depend upon the Indians to carry them down the mountain to the railroad. Indians aren't dependable like our mail carriers; they lose letters."

The explanation seemed not only to satisfy the judge, it dislodged a nameless fear that had fleetingly shadowed her own mind. "Most likely Father doesn't get some of the letters we write him, either, but we keep on writing to him just the same."

"When Dad gets home I'm going to ask him to buy me a bicycle like Dinky Smith's," Alan informed the judge between spoonfuls of ice cream. " 'Cept mine's going to have a headlight so's I can ride in the dark."

"Anybody in your party care to have another dish of ice cream, Jedge?" the waitress rested her hands upon the back of Jodie's chair to inquire. "Choice of choc'lut or vanilla. Cherry's all out."

Though such an opportunity might never again offer, the children were forced to decline. "It's awful good," David told her, "but I can hardly finish what I've already got. Thank you just the same, though."

Of course it was their host who received their real thanks. Alan asserted that eating in a restaurant was better than a birthday party and next time he wouldn't eat any breakfast before he came. David shook the judge's hand with a boyish, "Thanks a lot, Judge Neal, it was swell!"

"Next time it's our turn to have you for dinner," Anne declared. "You and Mrs. Neal both. But you mustn't expect us to be very good cooks." Secretly, however, she was determined to serve a meal every bit as good as he had invited them to, no matter if it took a whole day to prepare.

He accompanied them to the bus station and when the bus rolled in a few minutes later, he swung Jodie aboard. The others required no assistance.

Anne stuck her head out the window for a last good-bye. "We're ever and ever so much obliged—for *everything!*"

That was another thing that was so satisfactory about Judge Neal, she thought, settling herself in her seat as the bus got under way. You didn't have to try to say everything out in exact words, you could trust him to know what you meant by *everything*—the mud on Mrs. Lloyd's clothes and how fair he had treated Davie. Honestly, she told herself, honestly Judge Neal was the nicest man she was ever acquainted with. Except of course their own father.

She concentrated upon the scene outside the window, two boys trying to teach a wobbly black and white puppy to stand on his hind legs. There was a thought somewhere at the bottom of her mind which she would not let herself think about, because it wasn't true. . . . Why, there might be a letter from their father in the post office this very minute, waiting for them to call for it. And if there wasn't, there was sure to be one next week.

"I'll bet Judge Neal knows more than Dinky Smith's father," Alan proclaimed across the aisle. "I'll bet he knows more than Dinky's father and Micky Moore put together, don't you, Dave?"

8

CAPTAIN PEGLEG

The next day was Friday and Alan was spending the afternoon at Mrs. Scott's, learning how to make sugar cookies. David was there too, but he was busied in the back yard. Mrs. Scott had offered to pay him by the hour to remove the nails from the shingles the carpenter had torn off when he put a new roof on her back porch. That done, he was to stack the shingles in neat piles in the garage for next winter's kindling. It was a piece of work which gave David satisfaction because it promised to pay better than cutting the grass or pulling up weeds.

Jennie Allen's mother had invited Anne and Jodie to drive to the country with her and Jennie to spend an hour or two with Jennie's grandmother. Anne sometimes wished they could live on a farm, it would be so enjoy-able. Although Springtown was next door to the country it was not at all the same as a farm. There were no hay-stacks to slide down in Springtown, no barnlofts to climb up into to trample the dry, windy-smelling hay and straddle the cross-beams so high in the air you hardly dared glance down for fear of losing your balance. Nor were there in Springtown any stretches of wood-land so dark and shady you could easily imagine your-self in the middle of a forest as primeval as the one in the poem about Evangeline.

This afternoon, however, since Jennie had worn a new plaid gingham dress to show her grandmother and didn't wish to get it mussed up, and Anne had Jodie to think of, the girls went no farther than the row of cherry trees along the orchard edge. It was plain to see that the cherries were ripe for picking, shiny dark crimson, such quantities of them thrusting in innumerable bright clus-ters among the green leaves the sight was altogether tantalizing. For not a single cherry grew within arm's reach. The upper branches were laden with the luscious red fruit, but the lower ones bore nothing except leaves.

"No wonder Grandma didn't offer us a piece of cherry pie!" Jennie exclaimed as they circled the trees for a second time, hoping to spy a few cherries on a lower bough. "The birds eat them all. It's a shame. Just look at them!"

"Look at the robins if you want to," Anne replied, jumping down from the fence post she had mounted in a vain attempt to seize an overhanging bough. "I wouldn't give them that much satisfaction. It makes my ears burn just to imagine the dreadful remarks they're making about us, all of them talking at once. You don't have to understand bird language to know they're calling us bad names. You'd think the trees were their private property and we had no right to be here, the way they scold us.

"Stick your fingers in your ears, Jodie. Show the greedy old robins you're not listening."

Cheated of the cherries, the girls pulled themselves each a stem of rhubarb from one of the broad-leaved plants in the garden to appease their appetites—a short, pinky-colored stem for Jodie and long, greenish-red ones for themselves.

"Let's go down to the duck pond and see if there are any babies," Jennie suggested, making a wry face because the rhubarb was so sour. "Last week they hadn't hatched out yet."

Though the pond had shrunk to less than half its size for lack of rain, it was still large enough to float a dozen ducklings, the muddy water reflecting in darker, broken shades the downy yellow balls that paddled on its surface. The mother duck flapped her strong wings and menaced the girls with a hiss lest they approach too near, somehow contriving almost in the same instant to sound an urgent quack-quack of warning to her babies.

"We're not coming any closer, it's too muddy," Jennie informed her. "Nor we wouldn't hurt your children, you old fuss-budget, even if we picked them up in our hands."

Jodie begged to have the ugly duckling pointed out to her, the one Anne had told about in the story.

At first they thought they must disappoint the child, for every member of the small, yellow-hued flotilla looked precisely as perky and flourishing and pleased with himself as every other member. They went scooting across the shallow water as lightly as though they were sliding upon ice, pausing now and then to blink their beady eyes and open and close their shiny yellow bills for all the world like their mother snapping up a dragon-fly. They were such fun to watch that Anne hoped Jodie might forget about the ugly duckling and thus escape disappointment at not seeing him.

It was Jodie herself, however, who spied the outcast just as Jennie was remarking that maybe they ought to return to the house, not to keep her mother waiting. He was brownish-colored and droopy, half hidden under a cocklebur bush on the far side of the pond.

"He feels bad 'cause they won't play wif him 'cause he's ugly," Jodie observed sagely. "He hurts in his feelings, I 'spect.

"Don't cwy, baby duckling," she called at the top of her voice to cheer him up. "You're going to be a gweat big white swan. It says so in the stowy."

"Most likely what ails him is he probably ate something he shouldn't," Jennie remarked under her breath to Anne, speaking no doubt from experience. "Though naturally I wouldn't tell Jodie so, to spoil the story."

But Anne, though she did not say so, was of the opinion that Jodie might understand better than Jennie what thoughts the brown duckling was thinking. For Anne herself sometimes felt that she didn't want to grow up, because she had such plain brown hair and freckles on her nose. How could you expect anyone ever to fall in love with you and do brave deeds for your sake unless your were beautiful?

"If you children had dawdled a minute longer you'd have had to walk home," Jennie's mother told them as they rounded the corner of the house. "I'm ready to step on the gas." Which was not literally true, since she was still loading a basket of roasting ears and new potatoes and a chicken for Sunday dinner into the car.

"Whatever have you been doing all this time, Jennie? It's after five o'clock. You know your father will be sitting on thorns if I don't have dinner on the table for him at six."

"We haven't been doing anything, have we, Anne?" Jennie, who knew her mother never meant it when she talked like that, pretended for her grandmother's benefit to be aggrieved. "We only walked around a little bit. Nor she didn't tell us she was in a hurry, did she. Grandma?"

"Don't be so impatient, Lettie." Jennie's grandmother reproved Mrs. Allen as though she were still about Jennie's age. "You'll hurt the child's feelings, talking to her like that. What difference does it make, a few minutes more or less?

"Nor I've no intention of letting you start until these children have had a bite to eat, Lettie. Growing children require nourishment."

"You bet we do, Granny! We're starved to death, all three of us." Jennie rubbed her smooth, sun-reddened cheek against her grandmother's old wrinkled one and blinked impudently up at her mother. "Mum wouldn't care if I famished."

It would be wonderful to have a grandmother, Anne thought. The things Father told about his grandmother sounded just like Jennie's, always taking the children's part and feeding them cookies and pie and whatever else they liked specially to eat, and thinking they were smarter than other people's children and didn't have any faults.

It was cherry tarts and glasses of fresh milk that were set out on the kitchen table to refresh the three girls. Jennie's mother munched a tart too, though she protested that she shouldn't, it would make her gain a pound and she was trying to lose weight.

"There's two pies in a cardboard box in the back seat," Jennie's grandmother informed the girls as they brushed the crumbs from their dresses ready to depart. "One for you to take home, Anne, and the other for Jennie. I sent the hired man up a tree on a ladder this morning, trying to get ahead of the birds."

When Anne told her how pleased the boys would be, because cherry was their favorite pie and they hadn't had one since Mrs. Malet left, Jennie's grandmother said she only wished she had known it sooner so she could have baked an extra one for them. Anne didn't know any old lady she liked as much as Jennie's grandmother.

It was almost six o'clock when Mrs. Allen deposited Anne and Jodie at their front door. "If the boys complain because supper is late," she advised Anne with a twinkle, but half in earnest too, "tell them you'll hold out on the pie. That's the threat I intend to quiet Jennie's father with."

Jennie was optimistic. "Dave's not helpless 'round the

kitchen like Dad, is he, Anne? Most likely he and Al already have got supper on the table. You can bring out the pie for a surprise."

Jennie's optimism proved to be hardly in accord with the facts. Indeed it was quite to the contrary, as Anne soon discovered. Not only was supper not on the table, but the two boys were sprawled at their ease in the living room entertaining a guest.

"Hi, Anne," David hailed her, "we've got company. Captain Pegleg's come to visit us. Hurry up and cook supper. We're hungry."

She was so taken aback to find an unexpected guest awaiting her, a person she had never seen before, that for a moment she felt quite blank. As she summoned her wits to remember her manners, it occurred to her who he must be. Yes, of course, he was the one who had hired David to peel onions and taught him to tie the figure of eight. But what was he doing here? Why wasn't he with the circus where he belonged? And why hadn't David told her that he had invited him for supper?

In the kitchen Anne tied on an apron and took stock of supplies. She knew before she looked that there remained only three cans upon the pantry shelf. She had intended to open one a day until the money came next week from the oil company. It would not do, however,

to serve a guest a scanty meal, especially a guest who was accustomed to the bountiful kind of table the cooks at the circus provided.

Really, it had been most inconsiderate of David to invite the captain now. David knew as well as she did that they must not go into debt at the grocery store. Well, if anyone grumbled because they had to live on boiled rice and potatoes for the next few days, it wasn't her fault.

Nor was there a crumb left over to warm up for the next day. For such a thin, small, puny-looking man Captain Pegleg had a surprisingly hearty appetite. He wasted no time in table conversation, applying himself strictly to his plate, and he took second helpings of everything, sometimes even before they were offered.

"You mustn't have had a very big lunch," Alan observed as the captain scraped the bottom of the dish of creamed salmon. "That's three helpings you've had of that. I and Dave only took one 'cause we're saving room for pie."

If Captain Pegleg was embarrassed by Alan's remarks, as Anne feared he might be, he did not show it.

"Di'n't have no lunch, and footed it seventeen miles," he commented briefly between mouthfuls of salmon and beans. "Couldn't thumb a lift from nobody, they wuz all speedin' so 'tarnal fast." He reached across the table for the last slice of bread on the plate. His sleeve was frayed and patched, Anne noticed, the stitches so long and crooked he must have sewed them himself.

"Why didn't you ride on the bus?" Alan persisted in putting questions although Anne shook her head at him not to.

"Elyphunt stepped on my pocketbook."

While Alan pondered the meaning of this enigmatic statement, David spoke up to inform Anne that the captain was on his way to the Caribbean. "He's going to ship for the Spanish Main where he can take things easy. He's tired of working for the circus. It's not what it's cracked up to be."

"Mind you, I don't say but it might do for landlubbers as ain't used to nothin' better." Captain Pegleg shoved his plate away, to indicate his readiness for the next course. Following his example, Alan and Jodie promptly gave their plates a push.

"All I'm sayin' is it ain't no life for an old sea-dog like Cap'n Pegleg."

A little later, when Anne inquired whether anyone would have another piece of pie, he said yes, thankee, if she had it to spare, he'd be much obleeged. He was partial to cherry pie, and this one was mighty tasty.

The boys' faces fell as they watched in silence while he set fork to a second piece. A light kick under the table had conveyed a warning from Anne that they must not ask for another, there wasn't any more. Nor could Anne herself smother a slight sense of disappointment at seeing the last cherry disappear. She had cut her and Jodie's pieces extra small to have some left over for tomorrow.

As Anne was washing the dishes David stuck his head in at the door to whisper that if it was all right with her, Captain Pegleg would like to swing his hammock in the garage for the night.

"The garage is no place to sleep in, tell him," Anne whispered back. Perhaps she ought to let him have Mrs. Lloyd's room. But if she did, she would have to make up the bed and there were no fresh sheets because the laundry had not come. "The garage is filled up with old furniture. It hasn't been cleaned out in ever so long."

"I already told him, but he says that's what he wants. The garage, I mean. He doesn't want to be in anyone's way."

Anne unscrewed the pantry light bulb for the empty socket in the garage and sent Alan upstairs to fetch a pillow and a cotton blanket, though the captain insisted that his coat would be cover enough on a night warm as this. Then she turned on the light on the back porch for him to see his way down the yard. David led with the pillow and Alan trailed behind with the folded blanket.

The sun had set long ago, but threads of color still floated upon the western sky, fading rose and gold and dusty amethyst. The shadows were thickening and darkness would soon take over. His duffel bag humped over his back, Captain Pegleg looked like a gnome in the dusk, only a size or two larger than the ones who had befriended poor Snow White. It did not seem very friendly not to invite him to sleep in the house. For a minute or two Anne was almost of a mind to call him back. What kept her from it she hardly knew.

"He's got a lucky stone he traded from a sailor from India," Alan reported when he returned to the house. "It's green. He's 'most positive it's a nemerald. Ever so many performers at the circus tried to buy it, but he wouldn't part with it 'cause then he'd lose his luck. Don't you wish we had a lucky stone, Dave?"

"Did you know emeralds are worth lots more than diamonds, Anne?" David's eyes shone bright as Alan's at the marvels the captain had been imparting. "He says where he's been in Africa you can pick up diamonds off the ground. The natives don't think any more of them than pebbles, they're so common. Boy, I wish we could go to Africa!"

"Why didn't he bring some back with him?" Anne questioned as she herded the three children upstairs to bed. She was not at all sure that she believed Captain

Pegleg's stories. If they were true, how did it happen that he was so poor and shabby? "He could sell the diamonds and get himself a house and not have to go to sea."

"He doesn't *have* to go to sea," David corrected her in a louder tone than was necessary. Perhaps he sensed the doubt which she had not expressed in words. "He's going to sea because that's where he wants to go. He says it was mighty foolish of him ever to skip ship in the first place, even to join up with a circus.

"And if you want to know, he did fetch a whole ditty bag of diamonds with him out of Africa, didn't he, Al? But somebody stole the bag one night while he was asleep."

Alan bore solemn witness to the captain's lost treasure. "Di'monds big as hens' eggs," he said, measuring the size with both hands.

"In the morning he's going to show me how to tie a carrick bend and a Matthew Walker," David boasted. "Is it all right for us to use up the rest of that old clothesline, Anne?"

But when the morning arrived, Captain Pegleg was gone. Pillow and folded blanket, with the light bulb resting on top, lay in a neat little pile upon the back porch beside the bottles the milkman had delivered while the household still slept. Only a burned match and a dark ring on the old chair in the garage where the visitor had tapped the ashes from his pipe remained to show that a traveler had here found lodging for a night.

"I 'spect he was in a hurry to catch his ship," Alan surmised. "I wish he'd waited to show us how to do those knots. He promised to, didn't he, Dave?"

Anne could see that David's disappointment went deep. And indeed she herself thought it was not very polite of the captain to go off like that. Nor was it right of him to tell David about those knots and then not to keep his promise.

"Most likely he didn't want to put us to any trouble about breakfast," she made excuse for him, to spare David's feelings.

"Playing Indian is more fun than sailors anyhow," declared Alan, giving the garage door a sudden push with his foot to bang it shut. "The tadpoles don't like it when we build a raft on top of their water."

9

BAD NEWS

The dinner which the children prepared for Judge Neal and his wife was a great success. Even David, though against Mrs. Scott's advice he had argued long and loudly for roast turkey, had to admit that Anne's meat loaf tasted good. Nor was this opinion due solely to the fact that it was he who arranged hard-boiled egg to look like daisies on top of the loaf, like the picture in the cook book.

Every member of the family had a share in the dinner. The boys peeled the potatoes for Anne to scallop, and Anne helped Jodie with the peas and Alan with the lima beans. When Micky Moore came by early in the afternoon and saw what interesting preparations were under way, he volunteered to stay and lend a hand. This was not a good time for fishing anyhow. Catfish won't bite when the sun is high.

There wasn't anybody who could do a smoother job of skinning tomatoes than Yours Truly, he told Anne. He had learned how to loosen the skin by scraping it with the back of a knife when he made salad for the Scout Jamboree. Only she must promise not to let on to his mother how handy he was at cookery because then she might expect him to do it at home.

It was too bad that Anne was not planning to have Irish stew for dinner because Micky would have been glad to make it. He had quite a reputation among the fellows for stew. Even the scoutmaster couldn't make better. And as for flapjacks—at thought of the mouth-watering delicacies Micky closed his eyes with rapture and rubbed an expressive hand across the blue-checkered apron Anne had tied about his middle—he was a sure-enough sharp at flapjacks. He could toss them three feet high in the air, almost, and catch them on the griddle every single time—almost.

Micky was taller than Anne, and older, and next year he would attend high school. David and Alan hung upon his every word.

"Teach me, Mike, will you?" begged David, proud to

be scraping carrots at the same table with so accomplished a chef. "To toss flapjacks, I mean."

When your sister insists that nobody is going to call you a sissy for learning to cook, that's one thing. But it is an altogether different thing to have the shortstop on the school baseball team boast in your presence of his skill with frying pan and stew pot. And what was more, Micky didn't care who knew he liked to cook, so long as his mother did not find out. Which was only natural, for what is fun to do on a hike or at somebody else's house very often seems just plain hard work when it must be done at home.

If the labor of dinner-getting was quickened by the extra pair of hands, it was also lightened by talk of boys' affairs. The overnight hike the Scouts were planning to an abandoned mill, the leak in the waterworks dam which took a whole day to repair, and the stray calf that scared old lady Towers out of her wits when she went out in the dark to see what was causing such a commotion in her hen house—all this and much else which was news to the Todd family, Micky regaled them with.

Hearing him talk made Anne wish she were a boy. There were so many things a boy could do which girls couldn't. Not that girls wouldn't be able to, but they weren't allowed to.

"This plate with the three slices of tomato exactly the same size is for the judge," Micky pointed out. "It's got rufflier lettuce than the others.

"This one's for his wife. I took special pains with it too, but one of the slices turned out a little crooked. It won't matter whose places you put the rest of the salads at. They're all about the same."

"If you'd measured them out with a ruler and compass they couldn't look nicer. That's because you're so good at arithmetic, Micky," Anne declared, brushing the flour from her hands to admire each plate in turn. "If Judge Neal asks who made the salad, Jodie," she gave mock command, "don't you or Alan tell him. I'll take all the credit myself.

"I wish you'd stay for dinner, Micky. Micky would like Judge Neal, wouldn't he, Dave? And he's just as easy to talk to as anybody in Springtown."

"Thanks." Micky grinned and shook his head. It was a well-shaped head with a thatch of sand-colored hair. His hazel-colored eyes always wore a rather surprised look, as if they were astonished to find themselves keeping company with the brownish freckles which marched across his nose.

"I can't stay." He yanked off the checkered apron Anne had given him to wear, now somewhat vegetable-stained and spotted with salad oil, wadded it up and tossed it across a chair. "I've got things to do."

"There's plenty of time to go home and change into your good suit if that's what's on your mind," Anne urged. But he was not to be persuaded. He did, however, accept a handful of animal crackers and a couple of gingersnaps to tide him over the hour or two until suppertime.

The few minutes that remained after the table was set, before the guests arrived, seemed longer than all the preceding hours of the day put together. Dressed in their Sunday best, the two boys with their hair parted on the side and slicked down flat, Jodie with her blond curls as neat as Anne could comb them in a hurried five minutes, the three children sat perched upon the edge of the davenport in the living room to await the company.

Anne sat on a straight-backed chair where she could keep an eye upon the clock in the hall. She was wearing the pink linen dress Mrs. Malet had made her to sing in the school chorus. Pink was Anne's favorite color for dresses, and Mrs. Malet said it was a good choice because it set off her dark hair.

"Remember when you remove the plates to take only one at a time," she felt it was necessary to remind the

boys again. "And look where you're going so you don't bump into each other.

"Jodie, you'll be a good girl and not take such big bites, won't you? Little girls don't look nice with their mouths stuffed full. Nor boys either, Alan. She learned it from you."

"What if they don't come?" David was beginning to worry. The very same question had already knocked more than once at the back of Anne's mind. "They might think it was some other day."

Alan made an expedition to the hall to look at the clock. "It's five minutes to six and they're not in sight yet," he announced, so much in the manner of Mrs. Lloyd proclaiming "I told you so!" that Anne was half convinced the family was doomed to disappointment. "I'll bet we have to eat the ice cream all ourselves."

With each slow-dragging second the atmosphere grew less festive. Silence took over the room. The clock began to strike the hour—*one—two—three—four—five—* But before the sixth stroke chimed upon the air, uncertainty had flown out the window. A car had come to a stop in front of the house.

"Don't forget when you shake hands to give your right one," Anne gave Jodie last-minute instructions as they hurried out to the front porch to welcome the guests. "And be sure not to put your elbow on the table.

"Nor your elbows either, Al and Davie, it's not good manners." In her anxiety over the family manners Anne forgot to worry about whether the dinner would taste as good on the table as it had when they sampled it in the kitchen.

Mrs. Neal offered her services, but fortunately Anne

could assure her that everything was ready to dish up. She and David could manage between them, thanks just the same. Anne liked her at first sight, though of course she would have liked her anyhow because she was Judge Neal's wife.

She was not very big and there was gray in her hair, but her eyes shone so bright and lively behind her glasses and she stepped so quickly that she did not seem the least bit old. Not even as old as Mrs. Scott. Jodie took to her almost immediately, perhaps because her voice was quiet, Anne thought. Or it may have been the friendly way she smiled, or perhaps because she was wearing such a pretty soft blue dress. It was a relief not to have Jodie hang her head and refuse to speak. Mrs. Neal might have believed the child was pouting when she was only being bashful.

"I shelled the butter beans," Alan leaned across the table to whisper to the judge as the plates were being served. "The peas are Jodie's."

"Then I shall certainly demand seconds of both," Judge Neal replied in a stage whisper behind his hand, as though he and Alan were conspiring together. "See to it that I get the lion's share, will you?"

Alan fell to giggling and almost choked on a bite of bread, partly because it was so funny to think of a big fierce lion eating peas and beans and partly because it was so flattering to have a joke made especially for him. Jodie giggled too, just to be sociable, although she had no notion what was funny.

Mrs. Neal praised the meat loaf. When she learned that Anne had made it, with David's assistance, and that it was only the second one they had ever done, she would hardly believe it. It was the best she had ever tasted. Would Anne mind giving her the recipe? Anne promised to copy it out for her, but Mrs. Neal must be careful not to have the oven too hot, because the loaf would cook too hard on top.

It was so enjoyable to sit at the head of the table and be hostess, with everyone joining in the conversation and having a good time, and everything tasting as savory as if Mrs. Malet herself had been there to cook it, that Anne could not help thinking it must be more fun to be grown-up than she had realized. Because if this was what it was like, she wouldn't mind being grown-up and entertaining company almost every evening. Though of course not during the daytime. She wanted to keep on being her own age during the daytime.

Judge Neal inquired whether David still maintained his position as chieftain, and what exploits the tribe was now planning.

"We've not been doing Indians lately," David informed him. "We haven't had time. We had to build a raft and practice knots. Figure of eight and granny and slip knots mostly. Sailor knots, I mean, in case you don't know. But now we don't know any more kinds to practice.

"A friend of mine, a sea captain, was going to teach me a carrick bend and how to splice so I could show the other fellows, but he didn't. He forgot to, I guess." It was the first time Anne had heard David refer to Captain Pegleg since the visit he had made them. It must mean that David was getting over his disappointment that he could sound so casual.

"Anyhow," he continued earnestly after he had supplied Jodie with a clean butter spreader from the buffet drawer to replace the one she had dropped on the floor, "anyhow I think the fellows would rather go back to being Indians. At least I would. And so would Al. Because once you finish building your raft there's not much you can do except knots. Indians have more choice."

"That is exactly my opinion," Judge Neal agreed with him. "There was a time when I was a boy in New Hampshire I thought I might take to the sea myself, but I settled on the law instead. And I don't regret it. From what I have heard since, a sailor's life is not so adventurous and gay as it is popularly supposed to be."

In spite of Anne's protests, Mrs. Neal insisted that the dishwashing be turned over to her and the boys, with

Jodie as first assistant. She would not consent to Anne's rinsing off the plates and letting them stand until morning. It always takes twice as long to do dishes the next day. Besides, there was something which her husband would like to talk over with Anne, if Anne was willing.

Whatever Anne may have felt of relief at not having to clean up so many dishes and pans soon faded. From the way Judge Neal smiled at her when she joined him in the living room she could see that he was worrying about something. It was the kind of smile that people put on to make you believe everything is all right when it isn't. They can make their faces crinkle up to deceive you, but not their eyes. That was how Judge Neal was looking at her now, with a sort of trying-to-be-cheerful smile.

Something, Anne was suddenly aware without knowing how she knew it, something must have happened. . . . Something which concerned her and the children. And whatever it was, it was unhappy.

She wished she did not have to know about it. She wished she were back in the kitchen talking and laughing with the others, and that it were Mrs. Malet instead of herself who was sitting here on the green-upholstered davenport opposite the judge in the deep winged chair. Or if only Father were at home! If Father were here Judge Neal would tell him and not Anne, and Father would take care of it and she would not have to be responsible.

"I wonder, Anne, whether you and the children have ever thought of going to stay with relatives for a time?"

It was an easy question, nothing to be disturbed about. Yet there was a part of Anne's mind, sharpened by apprehension, which suspected that the query might have an inner, hidden purpose.

"Yes, sir," she replied breathlessly. "When Father was being sent to Ecuador we talked about it. But we decided not to. I mean Father and Davie and I decided. The others were too little." As she spoke, it began to seem more like an ordinary, everyday conversation. "If we went to live with Aunt Mary and Aunt Sue we'd have to be separated, and none of us was willing to be. Why, we might not even have seen each other until Father got back, because Aunt Mary lives in Texas and Aunt Sue moved to Oregon. Father didn't want us to be separated either, not if it could possibly be helped. So Mrs. Malet promised to stay with us."

"But she is not with you now?"

Anne had already explained, that day at the courthouse, why it was that Mrs. Malet had had to leave Mrs. Lloyd in charge. It seemed surprising that Judge Neal should have forgotten anything so important, especially as he was a judge.

Anne explained again about Mrs. Malet's two daughters. "But we expect her any day now," she concluded. "As soon as her daughter gets well enough to take care of the babies. They're twins, the babies are."

"I see." He nodded to show that he understood. But there was such a faraway, sober look in his blue eyes Anne had an uncomfortable impression that he had not really heard what she said, he was only pretending to listen. He was not interested to know about Mrs. Malet.

Anne's uneasiness returned. A heaviness seemed to be settling inside her mind that she could not shake off. If only Judge Neal would not be so serious! Why didn't he make jokes and laugh as he had at dinner? In the dining room she could hear David laughing about something as he put the silver away, and the others laughing in the kitchen. She wished she were out there with them.

"In the letter which Mrs. Lloyd sent me, she mentioned the fact that it had been several months since you had received word from your father," Judge Neal continued after a moment. "She thought it was not safe for you children to remain here alone."

So that was it! It was Mrs. Lloyd trying to make trouble for them again. On the instant something boiled up fiery hot in Anne's chest, clogging her throat and making it difficult to breathe—indignation perhaps, or resentment or dread, or perhaps all three.

She swallowed. "It's nothing to us what Mrs. Lloyd thinks." Anne was not being insolent or rude, and the judge knew she was not. It was the burning heat within her chest that could find no other outlet than words.

"It's none of Mrs. Lloyd's business. She has no right to interfere." But even as Anne spoke she was acutely conscious that Judge Neal would not be regarding her with such troubled concern merely on account of the housekeeper's letter.

"I wrote to the oil company to make inquiries. Perhaps I shouldn't have." It was almost a question, as though he feared she might think he was trying to interfere, like Mrs. Lloyd.

"Yes, you should have." Anne did not know exactly what she meant except that it is different when the person who takes a hand in your affairs is someone like Judge Neal, and your special friend besides.

"This morning's mail brought a reply." He frowned, not at Anne, although he was looking at her, but at some thought inside his mind. "It was not the kind of reply for which I had hoped. The news is not good, Anne," he concluded in the quiet, slow speech a father uses to steady a hurt child.

She clenched her hands into such hard balls the nails cut into her palms. "He's not— Father's not—?" She could not bring herself to pronounce the word. "They didn't say that Father—"

"No, the letter did not say that," Judge Neal replied gravely. Anne's sigh of relief was so sharp it might have been a sob.

Sitting beside her on the davenport, his head bent slightly forward to bring his tall height nearer hers, he covered her two clenched hands with one of his own. She could feel its kindness, and how warm and strong it was.

"The company has not given up hope. They have sent out a second searching party. To notify the families now might be premature, unless the families request information."

A kind of stiffness in Anne's thoughts prevented her from grasping all he said, or asking questions. It was as though she were not so much listening to the explanation as watching it take place inside her head. There seemed to be a light within her mind by which she could see into the darkness, a small, dim light like the one that burned all night in the upper hall so nobody would fall down the stairs. The figures she saw in her mind looked dark and shadowy as the jungle trees. She could not make out her father's face, but she knew it was he.

For Judge Neal was saying that her father and two other engineers had taken a group of Indian bearers and guides on a surveying trip into an unexplored section of the forest. When three months had passed and they were a fortnight overdue, a party had gone out from the camp to search for them. No trace either of the Indians or of the white men had been found. Six weeks ago the company had flown a new group to the region to continue the search.

"They must not have been looking in the right place," said Anne. It was like hearing herself talk in her sleep, her voice sounded so distant. "Or else they walked past without noticing them. They could, you know, the jungle trees grow so close together.

"And the vines and creepers hang down to the ground, so thick you can't see through. Sometimes you can't even cut your way through with a machete. That's a big kind of knife they have there," she explained, speaking faster and faster, not so much because she thought Judge Neal did not know, as because there was someone whom she had to keep talking to, to convince. Whether the someone was the judge or herself she hardly knew.

"They'll find Father, I know they will," she declared, almost as though it were Jodie she was trying to reassure. "Or if they don't, he'll find himself."

The numb, nightmarish feeling was beginning to drop away and she began to feel more like her own self again, only somewhat shaken and anxious. She looked at Judge Neal, to see whether he believed her.

"Most likely something happened, like one of the engineers breaking his leg, and the others couldn't go off and leave him." It was so reasonable an explanation she wondered why it had not occurred to her before. "Or maybe Father got sick and it's taking him a while to get well."

Judge Neal granted that her father might have fallen ill. But he still thought it might be better for the children to live with their aunts until Mr. Todd returned. It might be a matter of months, too long for Anne to carry the burden of housekeeping. Even after Anne had explained again about how the family committee voted to divide the work and help each other, he remained of the same opinion.

"Well, maybe sometimes they don't help me," she admitted reluctantly in response to his question. "But I don't work any harder than is good for me. Honestly I don't.

"And we want to stay at home to be here when Father comes. More than anything else in the world, that's what we want. Please, Judge Neal!"

Anne's cheeks were flushed pink as her dress, her gray eyes shone intense with hopefulness as they met his troubled blue ones, her voice pleaded with him to let her have her own way. He must let her. If it took all night to convince him, she was determined not to give in.

"Mrs. Scott next door will keep an eye on us, if you think a grown person ought to," she promised. "And we'll behave ourselves and not make trouble for anybody."

Although it was evident that he was not entirely won over to her way of thinking, he let himself be persuaded. He would give consent only until September, however. "If we have not heard from your father by then, it will be best for you to stay with your aunts this winter. It would be too great a strain for a girl of your age to manage a household and attend school."

"Oh, thank you, Judge Neal! Thank you ever so!" Anne smiled breathlessly up at him. "I knew you would!"

She did not argue about September. Mrs. Malet would return long before then, and then their troubles would be at an end. Mrs. Malet would convince him that it was important to keep the family together. Everything would be all right once Mrs. Malet was in charge again—and word came from Father.

It may have been that the judge could read her thought. "We must consider what is best in the long run for the children, Anne, you and I," he observed gently. "They are too young to plan for themselves. If the oil company should discontinue the monthly allowance it would not seem wise to use up your father's savings to pay a housekeeper."

The possibility that the monthly checks might come to an end was too alarming to be immediately accepted. "Oh, I'm not worried about that," she asserted, but her voice was not quite steady and her eyes grew dark with misgiving. "We'd be able to manage somehow, I'm positive we would. Nor I wouldn't spend what's in the bank. It's for college, Father said."

"You are a plucky girl, Anne," said Judge Neal. "And what is more, you have a good head on your shoulders. I am proud to have you for my friend."

The unexpected compliment—really two compliments, as she realized with a momentary shock of heady pleasure—had a tonic effect. The disheartenment, which had briefly threatened to overwhelm her, withdrew. Hope sprang up again. When a person like Judge Neal tells you he is proud of you, you can't help believing in yourself.

Anne wished she could keep from blushing. Other people's faces didn't get red as a beet when someone paid them a compliment.

"Let's not mention anything to the children, shall we?" she suggested, certain that he would agree with her. "And let's not tell anybody else."

There was another reason than not wishing to make

the children unhappy. Though the reason was not clear in her own mind, she felt obscurely that to tell others would in some unaccountable, mysterious fashion be equivalent to an admission that her father was really lost. He was not lost, she told herself, or if he was, it was only for a little while. He would come home as he had promised; he was safe somewhere. . . . Of course she was worried. But lots of things you worry about never happen at all.

She was certain that Mrs. Neal must know about the letter, because later as she was bidding them good night and saying what a delightful dinner party it had been, she patted Anne's shoulder in an encouraging, special sort of way. She did not mind Mrs. Neal's sharing the knowledge, in fact she was rather glad she did. It seemed to make her a more particular friend.

"Next time maybe I'll cook flapjacks for you, Judge," David remarked with studied nonchalance as they were seeing the guests into their car.

"Flapjacks!" Judge Neal exclaimed. "Did you say flapjacks?" He thrust out one foot as though he was on the point of returning to the house. "What about breakfast tomorrow morning?"

David was slightly embarrassed. "Not tomorrow. You have to wait till Micky Moore shows me how. Next week maybe."

10

MRS. MALET

It was a comfort to have a neighbor like Mrs. Scott, because there were times—especially when the housework piled up and the boys wouldn't behave themselves and do their share—when Anne had to talk to somebody to keep from getting discouraged. On more than one occasion she had been tempted to confide in Jennie Allen about what the oil company had written Judge Neal, but Jennie was not very good at keeping secrets, not even little, unimportant ones.

Micky Moore could be trusted not to tell anyone else, but the minute he stepped into the yard David and Alan always came running as though it were they and not Anne he had dropped in to see. As a full-fledged Scout with camping experience, Micky could have given her more practical information than Mrs. Scott about how persons who happen to get lost in a forest are able to make their way back to civilization. Only there was never an opportunity to ask him.

Despite Mrs. Scott's inexperience with forestry, however, she could think of more reasons than Anne for being hopeful. Nor was she the sort of person who makes light of your worries or pretends that you've no cause to be anxious. Which was why her reasoning carried weight. In the first place, as Mrs. Scott pointed out, it was not as though Mr. Todd were a child. He was a grown man, able to look after himself. And it was not as though he had never before been in a jungle wilderness. It was a piece of downright good luck too that he was an engineer, used to roughing it, instead of a bank clerk or an insurance agent who wouldn't have known how to cope with the situation. Moreover, even supposing he had broken a leg or fallen ill, as Anne feared, there were the other men to care for him.

After a talk with Mrs. Scott Anne always felt easier in her mind, so that she could enjoy a visit with Jennie Allen or settle down with a library book, if there was time to spare, without having thoughts of her father get all mixed up with the words of the story.

If Mrs. Scott were at home now, Anne would have

been seeking her advice about how to make the boys behave. Instead of doing the dishes as he was supposed to, Alan had washed only the plates and glasses. He had shoved underneath a pantry shelf the skillet David had fried eggs in last night and the double boiler in which the breakfast cereal had cooked. By the time Anne had noticed them, both skillet and boiler were stuck so hard she could hardly scour them clean, for of course Alan had not bothered to soak them in water.

David had flatly refused to assist with the upstairs cleaning. It didn't need it, he maintained. They had done it last week and nobody would see it but themselves anyhow. Besides, he had other things to do. The "other things," as Anne was well aware, were to show off the new nail-studded leather holster which had arrived in the morning mail. She almost wished Judge Neal had made David give the money to Mrs. Lloyd, if this was the way he was going to act.

When Anne sought to call a committee meeting to decide who was to help whom, David had only made an obstinate, whuffling noise and stuck his hands in his pockets and scraped his heel along the floor. So she knew she might as well give up. When David was obstinate, which fortunately was not very often, he was obstinate all over.

The boys were down in the pasture now, having fun

while Anne pushed the carpet sweeper back and forth and Jodie trotted in her wake with a dust cloth.

"I don't like dusting Alan's shelf," Jodie complained, wrinkling her nose and turning her head aside. "It smells bad."

Anne let go the sweeper handle to sniff inquiringly along the row of story books.

"It's a snake," Jodie explained, "a wattle snake he's keeping 'cause it died."

Anne was incredulous. "More likely it's one of his Easter eggs turned bad. There aren't any rattlers in Springtown." But when she pulled out the books to investigate, the remains of a snake lay exposed.

"It's nothing but a garter snake," she observed slightingly, returning to the sweeper. "Throw it out, Jodie."

Jodie hesitated, not from any reluctance to touch the uncomely object but because it was Alan's private property and she felt responsible. "He's saving it," she objected. "He wants to twade it for Dinky Smif's toadskin."

Anne was tired and it may have been that she was somewhat cross, having all the cleaning to do with no assistance from the boys. "I don't care what he wants. I won't have the smelly old thing in the house. Throw it out, Jodie."

Her nose pinched tight shut between dust-streaked

thumb and forefinger, Jodie laid ginger hold of the snakeskin and tossed it out the window.

"That's no place for it," Anne reproved her. "You know better than that, Jodie. I suppose you think I've nothing else to do but go downstairs and pick it up and dig a hole and bury it."

Jodie puckered up her face, breathing hard. Whether her feelings had been injured or she was in a huff it would have been difficult to say. Anne avoided the child's accusing gaze.

"That's enough, Jodie. I'll finish the dusting myself." Anne did not mean to sound sharp, but suddenly she felt so sorry for herself she almost wanted to cry. Nobody cared how hard she had to work to keep the family together, nobody was willing to help her. "Go play with the boys if you want to, Jodie. I'll do the work myself."

And without a word Jodie went, clattering down the stairs, banging the screen door, bouncing like a bright-colored, oversize India-rubber ball down the yard toward the pasture.

Anne jerked the sweeper across the floor and shoved it into the hall closet. There was a sound of footsteps on the back porch, and she had time only to dash a little cold water on her face (she wouldn't want whoever it was to think she had been crying, because she hadn't been, really), and run a comb through her hair before she ran down the stairs.

"Anybody home?" It was Micky Moore, in a clean shirt and blue overalls, with a pint bottle of what looked like molasses in his hand. "Hi, Nan, had lunch yet?" It was a nickname he sometimes called her.

"Because if you haven't, I'll make some flapjacks. Mom's gone to the Sewing Cirk but she said I could help myself to the maple syrup. I brought plenty for everybody. That is, if you want me to make 'em."

Most certainly Anne wanted him to! She would be glad to help, to learn how herself. The pancakes she and Davie had made last week had turned out so leathery even Dinky Smith's terrier had scorned to eat them. There must be some special trick about pancakes which wasn't in the cookbook.

"There sure is," Micky declared. "Even an old hand like me can't always count on turning the trick. Sometimes they get tough, or else they go wet and doughy in the middle. Must be something gets the matter with the flour is the only way I can figure it out."

Even with Anne to set flour and milk and baking powder and eggs within easy reach on the kitchen table, and hand him sifter and bowls and spoons of various sizes at command, the measuring and mixing were no small labor. One of the eggs crashed to the floor and had to be mopped up, milk dribbled over the edge of an over-full cup to trickle down a table leg, and flour rose in light clouds from the shaken sifter to settle upon Anne's bent head and Micky's clean shirt.

Conversation, such as it was, was chiefly monosyllabic. "Spoon!" Micky would demand, and "Tea or big?" she would offer him immediate choice, holding them up for him to take. Or "Milk!" he would give brisk order, tilting his sand-colored, cropped head toward the brimming cup, and a minute or two later as she emptied it thimbleful by cautious thimbleful into the bowl under his poised spoon, " 'S'nough," he would rap out, resuming his mixing.

Although he stirred with such force that little gobs of the mixture sometimes flew up over the rim of the deep bowl, there was nothing of the slapdash in his method. He concentrated upon his task, intent upon living up to his reputation as a master hand at flapjacks —perhaps even to outshine himself.

Absorbed in her rôle as Micky's assistant, Anne had long since forgotten her grievances against David and Alan. She was only glad when she brought out the skillet that she had noticed it in time to have it scrubbed clean before Micky appeared. She was scarcely aware that David's gang had broken out of the pasture to invade

the back yard, though from time to time she was conscious of voices.

With the sloping stride of movie-cowboys, accustomed to cover the ground astride a bolting broncho
rather than upon their own legs, the eight or ten little
boys advanced toward the house. David was in the lead,
right hand resting upon his nail-studded holster, ready
for the draw. A pace or two to his rear came Jodie,
somewhat out of breath because of the shortness of her
legs, but pointing the direction with outstretched arm.
Within a few steps of the house the group deployed to
the left, silent now and warily scanning the grass where
they set their feet.

"Hold, fellows!" David muttered a low warning and
lifted a hand to stay them. "Here's where I take over.
There's no use the rest of you risking a snake bite. I'm
used to rattlers."

"There it is," Jodie pointed out in a penetrating
whisper, "wight there under the window."

David must have taken aim, for on the instant there
echoed a shrill *bang-bang-bang* and then a staccato series
of louder bangs so noisy they drowned the thwacks of
Micky's spoon in the flapjack batter.

Anne glanced out the side window. "They've got an
old dead garter snake on the end of a stick, pretending
it's a rattler."

The boys were cavorting in circles, swooping and duck-ing, posturing like Indians in a movie snake-dance. With unflagging zest Dinky Smith pounded a heavy stick against the clapboards, a warrior thudding martial music on his drum. From time to time he uttered a howling shriek which might equally well have been a lament or a yelp of joy.

"Just kids," Micky remarked with a tolerant smile, "that's kids all over for you. Always pretending some-thing is what it isn't." He was too busy to look out the window. "I used to do a lot of pretending myself when I was their age.

"Sprinkle some drops of cold water on the skillet, will you, Nan?" he requested. "If they sputter a good deal, the pan's plenty hot."

"Shall I call Davie and Alan?" she inquired. "The table's set, all except pouring the water." But Micky preferred to wait until he had a supply of cakes ready to start with.

He did not toss the cakes. It took longer, he explained, and he was in a hurry because he was hungry. He con-sented to Anne's frying a few while he refreshed himself with a glass of ice water and sampled the gingerbread she had cut for dessert. The next time, when he showed Dave how to cook flaps, he'd toss. There was a fellow that Zeke Topping knew who could toss two at a time, one with each hand, and land them in two different skillets without a miss. Some day Micky intended to try it himself.

"Boy, I could eat a thousand!" David exclaimed a little later at the table, dousing his cake with maple syrup. "I'll say you're some prize flapjacker, Mike!" Somewhat to Anne's surprise David's feelings seemed not to be hurt because he had been neglected in the pancake lesson. Whether it was because the nail-studded holster was still so new, or because a hero like Micky could do no wrong, was anybody's guess.

"I'll bet if Micky wanted to he could get a job cooking for the circus, don't you, Dave?" Alan speared a larger bite upon his fork than Anne approved of. "I'll bet they'd pay him 'most a hundred dollars."

A voice at the front door floated into the dining room to startle the diners. "Is this the residence of a family by the name of Todd?"

It was the same question which the policeman had put a few weeks earlier, though in somewhat blunter language, but it could not be Officer Pettit this time. For it was a woman's voice, brisk and clear.

"Mrs. Malet!" There was a rush for the door, napkins flying, chairs shoved back, a general confusion of elbows, of brown heads and blond, and voices clamoring a welcome.

"We didn't know you were coming," Anne exclaimed as she unhooked the screen door for Mrs. Malet to enter. "You surprised us."

"Which was my express plan and intention," Mrs. Malet was gratified to inform her. She planted a hasty kiss upon Anne's cheek, thumped David resoundingly upon the shoulder, brushed a quick hand across the top of Alan's head, and swung Jodie off her feet with a bear hug.

Jodie squealed with delight. "Aren't you going to tell your old Rosie Malet you're glad to see her, my lambi-kin?"

But Jodie was too excited to say a word, clutching at

Mrs. Malet's hand and hopping up and down so close under-foot Mrs. Malet could hardly take a step.

"It's a pleasure to see you too, Micky." She shook his hand. "Looks to me as if you'd put on a couple of inches since I saw you. And you too, Davie, you're shooting up 'most as tall as Anne."

"Micky made us flapjacks for lunch," Anne explained, "and we've just begun. Wait till I set a place for you. Get Mrs. Malet a clean napkin, Jodie."

"Not till I wash off some of this train dust. It won't take a minute." And she went hurrying up the stairs with her bulging old suitcase while Anne and Micky hastened to the kitchen to cook fresh pancakes for her.

That the rest of them would have to satisfy themselves with cakes which had grown a bit clammy from standing was of no importance. But nothing short of perfection must be served to welcome Mrs. Malet.

"As tasty a flannel-cake as ever I put fork to," she commented as she took her place at table. "I couldn't have done as well myself, Micky. Is this your mother's recipe?"

With commendable modesty Micky replied that one or two of the other fellows could make them almost as good. It was a Scout recipe.

"Don't let anyone ever try to tell you that two babies are no more trouble than one," Mrs. Malet informed the table in response to Anne's inquiry about her daughter's new twins. "They make three or four times the amount of work. But I 'spect they're worth it," she added with an indulgent chuckle. "At least Marilla and her husband seem to think so.

"What I want to know is who's been doing the housework since Lilly Lloyd decamped? Neat as a pin the whole upstairs is, not a speck of dust under a single one of the beds, I couldn't help noticing."

"We do it ourselves." It was such a satisfaction to have her efforts commended that Anne felt more than repaid for her labors. "We formed a committee. Jodie too."

From David to Alan and back again to David Mrs. Malet's bright, bird-like gaze traveled. "That's the kind of brothers to have," she commented with a briskly approving nod. "Nobody shirking, everybody doing his fair share."

Under its coat of tan, David's face reddened. "Some times I didn't," he mumbled. "Anne did the most."

"Don't you pay any attention to what he says, Mrs. Malet." David's confession made Anne eager to overlook any slight shortcomings on his part. "He helped a lot, and so did Alan and Jodie."

Mrs. Malet assumed a plaintive expression. "Most likely next thing you'll tell me I can take my suitcase and go, I'm not needed, you can make out better without old Rosie Malet." Her sigh of self-pity—or perhaps a faint breeze from the open windows—set the yellow and orange-colored nasturtiums a-tremble in the center of the table.

The outcry that followed upon her mournful statement, the hubbub of protests and expostulations, and Jodie's half-scared grab at her hand to keep her from leaving them, would have persuaded even the most woebegone individual to cheer up and stay. And Mrs. Malet was anything but woebegone, her mournfulness being only sham, as even Jodie knew, put on to tease them.

Gazing at Mrs. Malet across the table, so plump and

capable in her green-sprigged summer dress, so homely and familiar and altogether comfortable to have around, Anne felt a sudden lump in her throat. . . . What if they couldn't keep Mrs. Malet after all? What if no August check came from the company and they had no money? For the check was already overdue. What if—

"Any time you want me to, Mrs. Malet, I'll be glad to show you how to make flapjacks," Micky was saying as he spread a thick coat of butter on his fourth one and reached for the syrup pitcher. "Just say the word when you're ready."

Mrs. Malet declared it was a bargain and she had witnesses and she would hold him to it.

11

IN THE TWILIGHT

One by one the days slipped away, sliding with the great golden sun down the rose-tinted western sky beyond the green wooded pasture and the level green cornfields. August was half gone.

Judge Neal stopped at the house one evening at sunset to invite Anne and the children to dinner on the following Monday. As he turned to depart he remarked almost as though it were an afterthought that he had received a letter from the oil company. Several members of the searching party had returned to the camp on the plateau, bringing with them one of the Indian bearers who had accompanied Mr. Todd and the other two engineers. The information the Indian could give was scanty, if indeed his word was to be trusted at all.

Two or three weeks out from the main camp—the Indian was vague about the distance—the surveyors had set up a temporary camp on an island in a river, where there was less danger from night-prowling beasts. Not long afterward a sudden flood had carried away most of the supplies and equipment. One of the white men had been swept against a boulder and injured as he struggled to save the skiff. When the floods receded and it was possible to swim to the shore, the guides had returned to the people of their tribe, leaving the white men on the island.

"Father and the other two engineers could follow the river back," Anne hastened to point out, as much to rally her own hope as to remind Judge Neal. "That's what Boy Scouts do. That's how you find your way back to civilization when you're lost in a forest on the mountains. You just keep going down the mountain beside a river or a stream till it brings you to a house or a road. Father knows better than Boy Scouts what to do because he's used to it." She was afraid to stop talking lest Judge Neal might say it could not be done in a jungle.

"Of course they couldn't hurry on account of the one who was injured. But maybe when they got tired they could ride in their skiff." She knew it would not be so simple as she was trying to make it sound, but she had herself to convince as well as Judge Neal and Mrs. Malet.

He nodded gravely. "Yes, I am certain your father would put his knowledge of the jungle to good use.

"Perhaps you might like to read the letter yourself, Mrs. Malet," he said, taking it from an inner coat pocket. And to Anne, "Tell David I'm looking forward to those flapjacks. Has he tried his hand at them yet?"

Anne hardly knew what reply she made, because instead of letting Anne read the letter too, Mrs. Malet carefully refolded it and returned it to the judge, who put it away in his pocket. They seemed to forget whose father it was, Anne told herself, her temper flaring up at being treated as though she were no older than Alan or David. But she managed to hold her tongue although her eyes smarted with the effort. Or it may have been tears of disheartenment which she could scarcely blink back.

And today Mrs. Malet had taken the bus to Centerville. Although her announced purpose was to shop for a new double boiler and cloth for dishtowels, Anne was almost certain she intended to talk with Judge Neal.

Usually she invited some of the rest of them to go along, but this time she had not mentioned it. When Anne offered to accompany her, Mrs. Malet said no, Jennie Allen was expecting Anne this afternoon and she must not disappoint her. Mrs. Scott would keep Jodie, and the boys could look after themselves in the pasture.

Jennie's aunt had sent Jennie several packets of dif-ferent-colored plastic cord from Chicago, with directions how to weave belts and a partly woven one for a sample. There was enough cord for belts for four girls, and Jennie had invited Ruth Belnap and Polly Smith as well as Anne. Ordinarily Anne would have been the first to understand the printed directions and make a start, but this afternoon she could not concentrate. She let the other girls choose their colors and she took what was left, not from any desire to be unselfish but because she could not interest herself in weaving a belt.

Her mind kept harking back to the letter Judge Neal and Mrs. Malet had not let her read. There must have been some news in it which they were keeping from her. Especially as Mrs. Malet had been in such a hurry to go to Centerville today. When Anne asked what else was in the letter, Mrs. Malet had replied that it had only mentioned the fact that some of the searching party had not yet returned to camp, having taken a different trail.

"That's reason for hope," Mrs. Malet had asserted. "You don't suppose for a minute they'd have tried a different trail unless they had good reason to, do you? Because I don't. Not in a jungle."

At the time Mrs. Malet's cheerfulness had been more persuasive than it seemed now that Anne was thinking about it as she wove the blue and green plastic cords in and out in a zigzag pattern. . . . If Mrs. Malet and Judge Neal were planning to send the boys to Aunt Mary in Texas and Jodie and herself to Oregon to Aunt Sue's, they were just wasting their breath. Because they were all going to stay right on here at home in Springtown, together.

If necessary, Anne would tell the boys. They would be just as determined as she not to have the family separated. She didn't care how obstinate and mulish the boys acted to keep from being sent away, just so they won in the end. They would none of them give in. Even if it should be a whole year before their father found his way back, she was determined that they would be waiting for him. Together.

"You've not done more than an inch on your belt," Polly remarked in surprise, uncurling her feet from under her on the porch swing to step across to compare her belt with Anne's. "Look how much I've done!"

"My fingers must be all thumbs." Anne pretended to be chagrined at her poor showing. It was a relief to have Mrs. Allen bring out a tray of lemonade and chocolate cookies, to distract Polly's attention. And it was a greater relief shortly afterward to have the weaving party break up and start home.

Anne sat up late to talk with Mrs. Malet after the

boys and Jodie had gone to bed. When Anne asked her outright, Mrs. Malet had to admit that she had been conferring with Judge Neal.

"We won't go to Aunt Sue and Aunt Mary, if that's what you decided," Anne announced defiantly. "Nobody can make us. We have to stay together because that's how we belong." So close underneath her defiance it threatened to break through and get the upper hand, was a dreadful fear that maybe she and the children would have to submit to the grown-ups' decision.

"Just wait till I tell Davie and Alan! They won't go either. And it would break Jodie's heart." A sob, half of anger and fear, half of grief which she could no longer stifle, forced its way out. "Oh, Mrs. Malet, I thought you were our friend!"

"There, there, child," Mrs. Malet said soothingly. "Let yourself go and cry. You're all worn out with worry, no wonder." She drew Anne close on the sofa and wrapped both arms around her as if to shut out trouble.

Anne laid her head upon Mrs. Malet's warm, comforting shoulder and sobbed. She could not help it; for the moment she was too unhappy and discouraged to try to help it.

"And Judge Neal's your friend too," Mrs. Malet continued after a minute or two, in the same mild, soothing tone. "He wants to make the best arrangements possible for all of you.

"If it weren't for not wanting to use up all your father's money, you and me and the children could go right on living here in Springtown. That's what I told the judge. I told him I could stay on at least a year without pay. I've got a little money saved that would tide me over, and I'd be glad to use it.

"But it takes considerable cash just to buy groceries and coal and shoes and clothes for four children, Anne. And as Judge Neal said, if it was all spent that way, there'd not be much left to send you to college when you're older. Your father wanted you all to have a college education. If you stay with your aunts the money can be saved." Mrs. Malet pushed Anne's hair back from her hot, damp forehead and gave her a clean handkerchief to dry her face. "But I'll let you make the decision, Anne.

"You don't have to decide now," she added quickly as Anne choked up again. "You've got plenty of time to think it over in—a week at least. It helps to sleep over a problem before you make up your mind."

"I've got fifteen days to decide in." Anne sat bolt upright and blew her nose. She had hold of herself again. "Judge Neal said till the end of August, and this is only the sixteenth. The other half of the searching party is bound to find Father almost any day now. You think they will too, don't you, Mrs. Malet?"

Mrs. Malet was turning out the lights and Anne could not see her face, but her "I hope so, child, I hope so!" was not very convincing.

Before Anne fell asleep she prayed harder than she had ever prayed in her whole life, the same prayer over and over again, "Please, God, please let Father come home."

Anne did not often think about her mother, but that night she dreamed of her. It had been so long since last she saw her, she sometimes could not remember very clearly what she had looked like. It had never really seemed as if her mother were not living. She had taken the train one morning to make a short visit to Anne's grandfather, who was old and ill. There had been a wreck, and she had not come home again.

At first Anne had kept expecting her, every time anyone stepped upon the porch, although she knew she was resting hushed and quiet under a blanket of green-growing grass in the churchyard. Then, as the weeks passed and she did not return, and the months went by and the years, her figure grew gradually fainter in Anne's memory, and the lonesomeness and emptiness she had left behind her faded and it was only seldom that Anne remembered to think about her.

But in her dream she saw her mother clearly, so near she could have reached out and touched her. She bent over Anne's bed, fair like Jodie and Alan, and slim and tall, smiling that same funny little teasing smile she used to smile when they coaxed her to tell what their birthday presents were going to be.

What happened in the dream Anne could not remember after she was awake, but all the following day she had a peaceful, contented kind of feeling as though everything were the way it used to be and she needn't worry.

Wednesday slipped away, and Thursday and Friday, and Saturday-Sunday-Monday, like beads from a broken necklace, too swift to stop. Now it was next week, and nine days were gone and only six remained . . . only five . . . four . . . three . . . two . . .

Mrs. Malet baked cookies and fried a chicken and bought a jar of fresh honey from the butter-and-eggs woman to spread on the hot biscuits, and kept up such a cheery flow of chatter that Anne had not much chance to think what day of the month it was. Mrs. Malet said why didn't Anne go down street to visit Jennie Allen for a little while after supper, since the boys and Jodie were playing hide-and-seek in Dinky Smith's yard? It would do Anne good to have a little walk.

But Anne was not of a mind to go visiting. She sat

upon the steps of the front porch with a library book upon her knees, repeating the words aloud to herself because it helped her to keep from thinking what decision she might have to make day after tomorrow. For deep within her mind she knew, although her heart was entirely against it, that she must sensible. She must save the money in the bank to send the children and herself to college.

She did not know what the story she was reading was about; she was only pronouncing the words one after another in the order they occurred upon the printed page. The sun had set but the light still shimmered upon the elm trees. The row of oaks along the sidewalk was darkening against the luminous eastern sky, the robins and cardinals had ceased their fluting, and mothers in the neighborhood were calling their children home through the twilight. It was growing too dim to distinguish one word from another upon the page, but Anne bent closer and strained to see.

A car was slowing to a halt in front of the house. They weren't expecting company; it must be a mistake. But the driver was climbing out to open the door for someone in the back seat, and reaching a hand inside to lift out a suitcase.

Anne's book slid unnoticed to the ground, her gray eyes widened, her heart almost stopped beating. For the figure which emerged from the car, tall and broad of shoulder and carrying one arm in a sling, was one she had so often during the past weeks longed to behold, striding in the old familiar way across the lawn to the house, that now for a moment she could scarcely be sure whether she was dreaming or awake.

"Father!" she cried, and again, "Oh, Father, is it you?"

Almost before the sound of her voice could reach his ear, she herself was at his side, breathless, half incredulous, kindling with wonder and swift joy.

His good arm encircled her, holding her tight as though he meant never again to let her go. "My girl," he said, lifting her chin with his hand to look into her eyes before he kissed her on each cheek. "My own Anne."

"They said you were lost." She pressed her face as hard as she could against the rough tweed of his coat to feel his nearness. "But I wouldn't believe them.

"Were you lost, Father?" she questioned in the same breath, anxious as a mother for the well-being of an only child. "And does your arm hurt much?"

"Not really lost," he assured her. "The Indians deserted, but we'd have managed to reach camp weeks ago if Jones hadn't contracted swamp fever." His easy, matter-of-fact tone and vague, comfortable gesture put the whole affair where it henceforth belonged, in the harmless past. Anne need never trouble her mind about it again.

"As it was, we were within a few days of camp when the remnants of the searching party stumbled on us."

"Father! Look, Al, look! It's Father!" an excited voice shouted in Dinky Smith's yard. "Run, Jodie, run. Oh, boy, it's Father!" And swift as homing pigeons David and Alan came winging across the street, with Jodie bouncing in their wake.

A wood thrush roused from his night perch in the lilac bush to add a stave of song to the general jubilation. But the song that sang in the heart of Anne was of a more golden music.